# THE CEO

NICOLA MARSH

Copyright © Nicola Marsh 2023
Published by Parlance Press 2023

All the characters, names, places and incidents in this book have no existence outside the imagination of the author and have no relation whatsoever to anyone bearing the same name or names and are used fictitiously. They're not distantly inspired by any individual known or unknown to the author and all the incidents in the book are pure invention. Any resemblance to actual events, locales, or persons, living or dead, is coincidental.

All rights reserved including the right of reproduction in any form. The text or any part of the publication may not be reproduced or transmitted in any form without the written permission of the publisher.

The author acknowledges the copyrighted or trademarked status and trademark owners of the word marks mentioned in this work of fiction.

First Published by Harlequin Enterprises in 2009 as TWO WEEKS IN THE MAGNATE'S BED.
World English Rights Copyright © 2023 Nicola Marsh

*All aboard...*

When museum curator Lana takes a well-earned vacation on a cruise ship, the last thing she expects is to work. But Lana's always been a do-gooder and it's hard to break the habits of a lifetime, even when her brash cousin Beth insists she has a makeover before her trip. Lana is a grumpy geek and proud of it. Until she meets fellow employee Zac, who's determined to tease her into playing...with him.

Zac has a secret and it's a doozy. With his company on the brink of collapse, he's determined to discover why, so going undercover on one of his cruise ships seems a sound plan for the CEO. But he doesn't count on being captivated by shy Lana and soon they're indulging in a steamy fling.

They're opposites and once the ship docks, they'll go their separate ways.

*Or will they?*

## CHAPTER ONE

As the taxi screeched to a halt, Lana Walker flung open the door and scrambled for her bags.

"Hey, slow down, you haven't missed the boat." The deep groove in the driver's caterpillar monobrow had been honed with years of practice if his glare was any indication.

The way she saw it, she may have arrived on time to board the Ocean Queen but she'd missed the boat metaphorically in every other way that counted—which was exactly why she was taking this trip.

She scrimmaged for the fare and darted a curious glance at the ship, spotting several officers in white uniforms on deck. Very impressive—and the ship wasn't half bad either.

A shadow loomed over the open passenger door as the driver dumped her suitcases and held out his hand. "Some people have all the luck. How about my fare, lady?"

Grouch. She resisted the urge to poke out her tongue as she handed him the money, stepped out of the cab, picked up her luggage, and headed for the escalators.

What would he know about luck? She'd worked hard for what she had, damn hard: five years as curator at Melbourne's premier museum followed by sixteen months as head curator at a notable museum in Sydney had been amazing, stimulating, and stressful. Sure, she had a stellar reputation in the industry and a gorgeous apartment in the beachside suburb of Coogee, but that was about it.

She didn't have a life.

No time-out, no socialising, no fun.

Over the next two weeks, she planned to change all that.

Though luck had played a part in this trip; if she hadn't won the cruise, she wouldn't have taken a vacation, considering her sad workaholic status.

As thoughts of work crowded her head, namely how she'd missed out on the opportunity of a lifetime courtesy of her crippling shyness, she stumbled at the top of the escalator and pitched forward, silently cursing the three-inch heels her shoe-crazy cousin Beth had loaned her for the trip. So much for the illusion of height giving her extra poise. It would be difficult to feign elegance when she landed on her butt.

Grabbing wildly at anything more stable than her, she exhaled on a relieved sigh as a strong pair of arms shot out, holding her in a vice-like grip.

"Whoa. These escalators are lethal if you don't concentrate. Too busy daydreaming, huh?" The smooth voice, with more than a hint of amusement in its husky depths, sent an unexpected shiver down her spine as she looked up into her rescuer's face.

Wow.

Seeing good-looking guys on a daily basis was a perk of her job. The museum was a haven for sexily scruffy archaeological students, attractive teachers, even the odd distinguished university professor. Yet this guy who pinned her with arms displaying a great set of biceps was so much more than that. Striking was more appropriate. Even sex-on-legs as brazen Beth would say.

Hypnotic eyes, a deep, cobalt blue, were fringed with long dark lashes any woman would envy, and those baby blues were focused on her, a teasing glint in their rich depths.

She inhaled sharply, unprepared for an intoxicating fresh, citrus scent that left her head spinning and not just from her near-fall. As for his lips curving upward with the hint of a smile, for the first time in her reclusive life she understood the term kissable.

All too aware she was staring—gawking, more like it—she lowered her gaze, only to be confronted by an equally intriguing sight, a broad expanse of tanned chest where the two top buttons of his shirt were undone.

She'd wanted to gain confidence, step outside her comfort zone, and experience new things this cruise; broaden her outlook to the extent she was never passed over for a business opportunity again, and had been thinking along the lines of dance lessons, lectures on exotic destinations, shore excursions, that sort of thing.

However, being held by this guy had her mind sailing down channels she'd never usually contemplate. Not a bad thing entirely, if taking this vacation had already affected her mindset. Maybe shy, geeky Lana—as she'd once overheard some colleagues call her—was already slipping into vacation mode.

Her heart thumping, whether in fear of her strangely errant thoughts or excitement at what they might urge her to do, she eased out of his grip.

He grinned, and typically, he had a sexy smile to match the rest of him. "Do I pass inspection?"

Great, he knew she'd been checking him out. Her subtlety skills were on a par with her wardrobe: shabby at best.

"What makes you think I was inspecting anything? You were holding me so tight I had nowhere to move, let alone look."

"Feisty." His eyes gleamed and the corners of his too-tempting-for-comfort mouth twitched in amusement. "I like that."

Heat suffused her cheeks as she struggled to come up with a comeback. She hated how she always thought of a great retort ten minutes too late. How was it she could bail up a slack student in a second, but right now her brain—a whiz at cataloguing priceless artefacts, leading tour groups and calculating storage data—was totally befuddled?

"Thanks for breaking my fall."

As replies went it was pretty lame. Pathetic, in fact; looked like her comeback skills had sunk to the same level as her flirting expertise: below average bordering on non-existent.

More embarrassed than she'd care to admit, she managed a tight smile, picked up her luggage, and turned away, striding toward the ship though her knees wobbled like just-set jelly.

"Watch your step," he called after her, his voice shaking with laughter.

She stiffened but didn't break stride, determined not to look back, refusing to give him the satisfaction. Besides, she could feel his stare boring holes into her back.

Her skin prickled at the recollection of those mesmerizing blue eyes twinkling at her, laughing at her, and she shook her head in disgust. She was such a novice when it came to interacting with the opposite sex.

"Live a little, Cuz. Let your hair down. Go crazy." Beth had encouraged. "You've got two weeks to cut loose, to be someone you wouldn't dream of being on land. Make the most of it."

Great advice, and it had sounded doable coming from her bubbly, confident cousin who bounced through life with a perpetual smile on her face. And Beth sure knew what she was talking about, considering her positive attitude had landed her Aidan Voss, the dreamiest husband on the planet.

As for Beth's other advice—"dust off the cobwebs, get laid"—Lana blushed just thinking about it.

It has been precisely one year, five months, and five days since she'd last had sex. Not that she was counting or anything. Besides, she'd have to date to have sex, would have to get emotionally involved with the guy to contemplate it, and she didn't trust her emotions anymore; not after what Jax the Jackass had done.

She tucked her old satchel under her arm tighter and headed for the gangway. Beth was right. While her professional life shone, her social life sucked. She had no confidence, no social skills, and no hope of being chosen for the museum's next overseas jaunt unless she learned to be more assertive, more outgoing, more everything.

Maybe this cruise would be exactly what a conservative curator needed?

～

ZAC WATCHED the petite brunette cut a path through the crowd, confused and intrigued. Most of the vacationers he met were dressed to kill and wearing enough makeup to sink a ship—no pun intended—yet she wore a simple navy suit bordering on severe and barely a slick of lip gloss, and had managed to capture his attention anyway.

He'd reached out to her in an instinctive reaction but once he'd held her, his synapses had short-circuited, because he found himself wanting to hold on way longer than necessary.

What was with that?

He'd lost any tender tendencies toward the fairer sex around the time Magda had done her chameleon act and he hadn't let a woman get close enough to sink the talons in since.

Unwittingly, his gaze was drawn to the diminutive figure striding toward the ship, head up, shoulders squared as if ready for battle. No simple walking for her. Instead, she swayed her hips in a natural, tantalizing rhythm in sync with her legs.

As for the way she'd glared at him...an image of feline hazel eyes and a full, pouting mouth sprung to mind. That mouth... He could've fantasized about it forever. As for that innocent schoolgirl-channelling-schoolmarm expression she had down-pat, he'd never seen anything like it.

When she stared at him with those striking burnt caramel eyes, she appeared wide-eyed ingenuous one second, ready to give him a severe scolding the next.

Fascinating, but he didn't have the time or the inclination to follow up on the first woman to pique his interest in ages. He had more important things on his mind, like ensuring he did a damn good job the next two weeks, before doing what he should've done years ago: accept his responsibilities.

# THE CEO

~

AFTER UNPACKING, Lana made her way to the Promenade deck and wandered away from the crowds along the railings to find a deserted spot with a clear view of the hustle and bustle below.

Circular Quay buzzed with activity: people waving as the ship pulled away from its berth, snapping the colourful streamers that bound it to shore. She had a great view from her vantage point, the Sydney Harbor Bridge on her left and the Opera House on her right as the ship sailed up the harbor, both landmarks imposing in the fading light.

The sound of low voices from somewhere on the deck above captured her attention. If she had a great view from here, theirs must be amazing.

"Looks like loads of single women down there. Half are here for flings, the other half hope to find a husband. It's the same every cruise," said an oddly familiar voice.

"Your job is to pamper those women, not judge them."

"Easy for you to say, buddy. If they see an unattached guy they're like piranhas circling their next meal."

Despite her intentions to ignore the conversation, this harsh judgment call made her look up. Standing above her, silhouetted against the Bridge, stood the stranger who'd saved her from falling earlier.

He wore a crisp, white uniform that accentuated his tan and made him look like the perfect advertisement for shipboard life. Deep furrows marred his brow as his gaze swept the crowd and she shrunk back, hoping she was hidden. She didn't want to be scrutinized by that disconcerting stare, not when she'd been eavesdropping, albeit unintentionally.

Mr. Nautical's generalizations about women had her

bristling enough to barge up there and give him a verbal spray—and if she had the guts to do that—yeah, right—she'd be winging her way to Egypt right now as the museum's spokesperson, not cowering under a deck hoping she wouldn't be spotted.

He was entitled to his opinion, she to hers, and right now, as her gaze darted overhead and she noticed those broad shoulders, deep blue eyes, and mop of unruly dark curls, her opinion screamed Neanderthal.

The band starting up drowned out the rest of his conversation and she stood still for several minutes, waiting for the men above to move so she could make her escape without being seen. After a few extra minutes of shuffling her feet to kill time, she sidled along the deck and took a few steps back toward an open door.

"Watch out."

The owner of the low voice stood so close a warm breath caressed her ear and she jumped and whirled around, her heart pounding as she stared into those familiar indigo eyes barely inches away.

"You startled me." She glared, desperately trying to hide her embarrassment for being caught eavesdropping.

"Sorry. Maybe if you watched where you were going we'd stop bumping into each other like this? By the way, I'm Zac McCoy."

He stuck out his hand, unaware she'd heard every word of his damning conversation and she'd like to keep it that way.

"Lana Walker." She placed her hand in his, unprepared for the jolt that shot up her arm as his fingers closed over hers, and she yanked hers out of his grasp, flustered by the residual tingle buzzing from her fingertips to her shoulder.

His eyes widened as he stared at her hand. Great, now

he thought she was rude as well as clumsy. Way to go with the first impressions. Not that she had any intention of impressing him after what she'd just heard. Not that he'd contemplate impressing him if she hadn't. Old clothes, minimal makeup, and boring brown hair weren't exactly designed to impress any guy let alone someone in Mr. Tall, Dark and Nautical's league.

"I need to finish unpacking, so if you'll excuse me?" As she pushed past him, her bare arm brushed his and the strange buzzing returned with a vengeance, spreading through her body and confusing the heck out of her. She had no idea why her body was behaving like this.

Okay, so that was a lie. Jax the Jackass had been her sole boyfriend, the only guy she'd ever slept with, and once he'd dumped her and she'd fled to Sydney, she'd had two less than memorable dates with co-workers. So her reaction to sailor boy had to be purely physical considering she hadn't been this close to a guy in seventeen months.

He nodded, his expression inscrutable. "I'll leave you to it. Nice meeting you."

Lana mumbled a non-committal answer and sent him a half-hearted wave, glancing over her shoulder as he walked away, her curious gaze lingering on parts it had no right scoping out.

She had a thing for guys in uniform. Always had, starting way back when a young sailor had given her a flower after she'd dropped an ice-cream cone and cried, a clumsy five year old who'd never forgotten her first crush. Her mom's warning at the time, to steer clear of men like that, hadn't meant much considering she didn't know what 'that' meant back then.

Now, seeing the white cotton outlining Zac McCoy's

butt as he strode away, she knew exactly what *that* was and it sent her scurrying for her cabin.

Banishing the encounter from her thoughts, she showered and dressed for dinner. Beth had crammed her case with designer dresses and shoes but Lana would never have the self-assurance to wear half the sexy stuff her cousin had packed so she settled for her one good dress, a plain black coat dress cinched at the waist, complemented with her cousin's sparkly ebony stilettos.

Beth had pestered her for a complete makeover, though the thought of a radical haircut and new wardrobe was way too intimidating for a girl who equated latest fashion with the occasional update of her tortoiseshell spectacle frames. So Lana had settled for a sedate trim to her blah-brown hair and swapped the specs for contacts, and Beth had been appeased when Lana agreed to take her shoe cast-offs.

As for the rest of Beth's advice on how to boost her self-confidence? She'd take it one step at a time in these damn uncomfortable shoes.

∽

Lana entered the Coral Dining Room and barely had time to notice the giant chandelier, the string quartet, and the gleaming silver place settings, before the maître d' whisked her to a table where two seats remained vacant.

She sat and let the other occupants introduce themselves, a couple in their forties and two other women, hoping they wouldn't expect her to make small talk. She was lousy in social situations like this, preferring to sit and listen than opt for idle chit chat.

She listened to their friendly banter while perusing the extensive menu and as the empty chair on her right was drawn back, her skin prickled. The type of skin prickle associated with the hives she'd been unfortunate to have several times when a strawberry came within a whiff of her.

However, this prickle had nothing to do with fruit. This time, something far more dangerous to her health—well, her peace of mind—caused her skin to flush and tingle.

"Hi, everyone. I'm Zac McCoy, the Public Relations manager. It's great you'll be joining me for meals at my table. On behalf of the ship's company, the captain, and the crew, we hope you enjoy your cruise."

Fate liked to play jokes on her. Maybe she should take out a lottery ticket and be done with it.

Resisting the urge to surreptitiously itch the flushed skin behind her ears, she tried to ignore her erratic pulse that shifted into overdrive the minute he sat down. She toyed with cutlery, pleated her napkin, and successfully avoided looking at him until the table introductions reached her.

"How are you, Lana?" He flashed that killer smile, blue eyes glinting with amusement.

"Fine, thanks."

That's it, slay him with scintillating conversation. For a businesswoman who gave presentations weekly—as painful as it was speaking in front of her peers—she was doing a marvellous job appearing like a brainless bimbo.

While the voluptuous blonde on his right distracted Zac, she couldn't resist sneaking a peek. Smooth, suave, and sexy, he was exactly the type of guy any sane woman would stay away from: a glib, good-looking charmer with the body of Adonis and a face designed to turn heads. Something like Jax with his people skills—and look how that turned out.

As dinner proceeded, Lana remained silent, toying with her food—a tender eye fillet smothered in a delicious mustard sauce she'd usually devour—and faking polite smiles. She'd never been a flirt and sitting next to a guy like Zac had her tongue-tied. Probably for the best, as she doubted he'd be interested in the latest marsupial display in the Australiana gallery or hearing her expound the virtues of digital cataloguing, though her reticence was barely noticed as he maintained a steady flow of conversation, captivating everyone at the table.

During dessert, a light chocolate soufflé that melted in her mouth, he turned toward her.

"You're awfully quiet. Maybe we should get to know each other better?"

His bold stare scanned her face and focused briefly on her mouth before returning to her eyes, admiration tinged with something more, something that made her heart go pitter-patter, glittering in those blue depths.

"Maybe, though I should warn you. I'm single and probably hungrier than a piranha."

His smile slipped as he dabbed at the corners of his mouth with a linen napkin, those vivid eyes never leaving hers for a second, and she blinked to break the hypnotic contact.

"You overheard me earlier?"

"Yeah, and your opinion of women on cruises sucks."

She silently applauded her bravado—fueled by indignation—while inwardly cringing at her outburst. Antagonizing him wouldn't be conducive to remaining unnoticed, which is what she'd hoped for if she had to sit next to him every night for the next fortnight.

His eyes deepened to midnight, dark and challenging, as he leaned toward her. "Care to change my mind?"

"And disillusion you I'm not the man hunter you think I am?" She eased back, needing some distance between them before she leaned into him and lapped up some of that delicious citrusy-sea-air scent he exuded. "Where's the fun in that?"

"I think it could be fun." His gaze dipped to her mouth again, lingered, before sweeping back to her eyes, and she flicked her tongue out to moisten her lips, tingling as if he'd physically touched her. "And seeing as you think I'm a judgmental idiot, it would take a lot of convincing." His voice dropped to a conspiratorial whisper. "Which could equate to *a lot* of fun."

"I didn't say you were an idiot."

He chuckled, a rich, deep sound that washed over in a warm wave. "You didn't have to. You've got very expressive eyes."

"Must be the contacts."

Her dry response garnered more laughter.

"Look, I'd really like to clear the air between us. I honestly didn't mean anything by what you overheard, it was merely an observation from working on these tugs too long."

She opened her mouth to respond and he held up a hand. "Yes, it was a sweeping generalization. And yes, I'm suitably chastened and I apologize. But tell me, Lana Walker, which are you?"

He leaned closer, so close she couldn't breathe without imprinting his seductive scent on her receptors. "Husband hunter or fun fling girl?"

She reared back, knowing now was the time to clam up like she usually did before she scolded him like her tardy students. But as her lips thinned into an unimpressed line, she noticed the teasing sparkle in his eyes, the cheeky smile playing about his mouth.

"You're trying to wind me up."

"Is it working?"

"No." Damn him, it was; not that she'd let him know.

"So I could say anything and you'd be totally immune to me?"

Immune? She could have a hospital's worth of vaccinations against suave sailors and it still wouldn't give her guaranteed immunity, the type of immunity she desperately needed the longer he stared at her with those twinkling eyes.

She tipped her chin up, faking bravado. "That's right."

"So I could say you intrigue me and you wouldn't react?"

"Nope." Liar, liar, pants on fire.

"What about the fact I think there's more to you than the obvious?"

She rolled her eyes. "That's the same as intrigue so you need to come up with a better line, sailor boy."

"Sailor boy?"

A slow grin spread across his face as she mentally slapped a hand over her mouth. Nicknames implied camaraderie. Nicknames implied fun. And there was no way she'd be foolish enough to ever contemplate having fun with him.

"Figure of speech." She pleated her napkin, folding it over and over with origami-like precision until he reached over and stilled her hand, setting her pulse rocketing as she tried not to flinch from his touch.

"What if I said I like you?"

Taking a great gulp of air to ease her constricted lungs, she frowned. "You're still trying to wind me up and you're good, I'll give you that."

She extracted her hand on the pretext of picking up her

wine glass, trying to come up with a way to end this conversation before she blurted exactly how wound up she was by his teasing. The nape of her neck prickled like a colony of ants had taken up residence under her skin and her blood flowed thick and sluggish, heating her from the inside out. Logically, it was merely a physiological response, a simple chemical reaction to the first guy to enter her personal space in a long time.

But logic wouldn't untie her tongue or stop the rising blush making her feel more gauche and awkward than ever in a social situation like this.

Smiling, he picked up his wine glass and raised it in her direction. "You do intrigue me. And I'm not trying to wind you up. Well, not much." His smile widened. "For some inexplicable reason, I've taken an instant liking to you despite your somewhat prickly exterior, and I've got two weeks to prove it to you."

Prickly? The cheeky son of a—

He chuckled and she knew he was winding her up again, trying to gain a reaction.

She bit her tongue, mulling over what he'd said. He'd taken an instant liking to her, huh? As if. If she believed that she'd believe the ship would sail into the horizon and drop off the end of a square earth.

He leaned forward to murmur in her ear. "I can promise it will be two very interesting weeks."

She stiffened, unable to think when he was this close. What was the best response? Ignore him? Berate him? Wait the requisite ten minutes it would take to think up a scathing comeback and put him firmly back in his place?

"What? Nothing to say? Surprising, from a woman with such strong opinions about me."

Sitting back, he fixed her with a smug smile, a smile

that said he knew how flustered he made her and how she was struggling to come up with a suitable response.

She should've ignored him, pleaded a headache, and left the table. She would've done it usually, slinking away from an uncomfortable situation then rueing her shyness. But his self-satisfied smile was too much, goading her to matching wits with him. He assumed she couldn't come up with a quick answer? She'd show him.

So rather than pushing back her chair and making a run for it, blood surged to her cheeks and her head snapped up as she fixed him with a scathing glare.

"Go ahead then, sailor boy. Prove it."

## CHAPTER
# TWO

Lana's eyelids creaked open at the crack of dawn the next morning. A converted gym junkie, she usually bounced out of bed early and hit the gym at six when the fitness fanatics liked to sweat through their first aerobics class of the day.

She'd never graced a gym let alone tried an aerobics class until eighteen months ago, all part of Operation Obliterate: obliterate her memories of Jax, obliterate the embarrassment of how he'd used her, obliterate the fact her first love had seen her as nothing more than a fling.

Ironically, not only had she become hooked on exercise, she'd become a qualified aerobics instructor for the fun of it. Madness, probably, but for the hour she jumped around every morning she was just like the rest of the sweaty women around her, when no makeup and casual clothes weren't a big deal.

After a quick shower, she donned her favourite Capri pants in urgent need of replacing considering the frayed cuffs, and a plain white T-shirt—she had a ton of the things as they went with everything—and slipped her feet into a pair of well-worn sling-backs.

Beth had shuddered when she'd seen Lana's casual outfits but she'd always been a comfort-over-style girl. Besides, she didn't adhere to the old 'dress to impress' motto. She used her brain to get people to notice her; discounting last night when her intellect had gone AWOL.

*Prove it*, she'd dared Zac, when he'd promised they'd have an interesting two weeks together. All very brave in the heat of the moment when she'd fired off a retort without rationalizing, but now, in the clear light of a perfect summer's day, her resolve wavered.

It was one thing to aim to build confidence by trying new things completely out of character, but challenging a pro like Zac to flirt with her could only end in disaster.

He'd pushed her, taunted her, until she'd snapped. He couldn't have known she'd react that way, because she still couldn't comprehend she'd done it herself. And while she now regretted her outburst, a small part of her was proud of her unusual flash of bravado.

Interestingly, the old, sensible, conservative Lana would've ducked her head, pushed her ancient glasses up her nose, and ignored him. She'd done it with co-workers at the museum before: scuffed her well-worn sneakers under the table, tugged on the hem of her favorite shapeless sweatshirt, and made a quick escape.

She'd always taken the safe route, always done the right thing, always focused on her career and nothing else. She was the diligent employee, the dependable colleague, the model girlfriend, the reliable cousin. And where had it got her?

She'd been dumped, then overlooked for a brilliant opportunity at work, and had come on this cruise for one reason and one reason only: to gain confidence socially and ensure she was never passed over at work again. If she couldn't rely on her job, the one thing in this world she knew she was good at, what hope did she have?

Maybe standing up to brash sailors and proving she wasn't a pushover fell into the category of confidence-building?

With a shake of her head—like that would dislodge the memory of making a fool of herself with a rash challenge—she headed for the Lido deck for continental breakfast. The food on offer was amazing and she helped herself to a plate of mango, strawberries, and pineapple before finding a table next to the floor-to-ceiling glass overlooking the Pacific Ocean stretching as far as she could see, the undulating swell soothing.

Her apartment in Coogee had an ocean view, though nothing as gorgeous as this. She'd deliberately chosen a sea view for its calming qualities and boy, had she needed it when she first moved to Sydney from Melbourne, hell-bent on leaving her past behind.

"Enjoying the view this morning?"

She glanced up, her pulse rate accelerating in an instant. Zac in a navy polo shirt and matching shorts, his hair recently washed and slicked back, resident charming smile in place, rivaled the ocean in the stunning stakes.

She took a sip of water, trying to ease the dryness in her throat. "Yes, it's spectacular."

He wasn't looking at the view. Instead, that steady, captivating blue-eyed gaze remained riveted to her. "Spectacular would describe it perfectly."

She blushed and glanced down, toying with the fruit on her plate rather than face his intense scrutiny. What made her think she could practice gaining confidence with this guy? He was a major player and she'd barely graduated from the little league.

"You really should try some of that mango rather than playing with it. It's succulent this time of year."

The way he said 'succulent' fascinated her; tripping from his lips, it almost sounded obscene.

"Shouldn't you be circulating with the passengers?" She speared a piece of juicy mango and bit into it, trying to appear casual yet anxious to fob him off.

As if in slow motion, he reached his index finger toward the corner of her mouth where a rivulet of juice had started to run and wiped it up.

Shaken to her core, she watched him lick the droplets of juice from his fingertip in a shockingly intimate gesture.

"Mmm, tasty." His smoldering gaze focused on her lips before sweeping back to her eyes, triumphant blue clashing with shell-shocked hazel. "You're right, I should get back to work. I can't be waylaid by one woman only, delectable as she may be."

With a cocky smile, he gave her a half-salute and sauntered away, the corner of her mouth still quivering from his sensual touch.

If that was his first foray into *proving it*, she was in trouble. Big trouble.

She devoured the remainder of her breakfast, eager to escape. Whenever she looked up from her plate, she caught a glimpse of Zac moving among the tables, talking to passengers. Their eyes met once across the crowded room and she looked away first, hating the heat surging to her cheeks, hating her inadequate coping with a light flirtation from a pro more.

The heat from her cheeks traveled through her body. She had to get out of here. After almost tripping in her haste to stand, she dashed for the door, head down, unwilling to tempt fate further. After virtually falling into Zac's arms at the top of the escalator when boarding, landing next to him at dinner, and running into him first thing this morning, it looked like fate was having a mighty big chuckle at her expense.

∿

Zac watched Lana bolt, hiding a triumphant grin as he flipped pages on his clipboard. He had her thoroughly rattled if that stunned, wide-eyed gaze was any indication when he'd touched her lips.

Maybe he'd pushed the boundaries a tad but he couldn't help it; he wanted to see if anything disturbed that cool bordering on haughty mantle she wore like a fine fur.

He'd disconcerted her last night to the point she'd thrown out that challenge, for he was in little doubt she would've never been that sassy if she'd been thinking straight. After all, a woman who turned up to a first dinner on a luxurious cruise liner wearing a drab black dress with oversized buttons, a god-awful belt, barely a slick of makeup, and rarely spoke wasn't exactly brimming with confidence.

Yet he'd wanted to tease her regardless?

Must be the pressure. He had a job to do, a spy to uncover, and some corporate espionage to bring to a screaming halt. His uncle was relying on him and he owed Jimmy, big time. He'd let him down once, never again.

Zac needed to concentrate on business, to convince everyone he was on the up and up. The success of his plan depended on it. Hell, the success of the whole damn company depended on it.

A company he now ran.

And concentrating on business meant not giving Lana a hard time, challenge or not. Though there was something about the spark in her eyes when she'd fired back at him last night, something about her wary-yet-indignant expression that had him wanting to delve beneath her prissy surface and discover the hidden depths.

Maybe if he unnerved her enough, he'd get to see the real her?

An interesting proposition but for now, work came first. Work was reliable, dependable, and never let him down. It wasn't clouded by emotions or changed when he least expected it. Work was the one constant in his life, the only constant.

Exactly the way he liked it.

∽

As Lana lounged around the Lido pool, she studied *Neptune's News*, the ship's daily planner, staggered by the array of activities on board: lectures on ports they were due to visit, wine tasting, art auctions, dance lessons, to name a few. She studiously avoided any activities with Zac's name next to them and finally decided on ballroom dancing, something she'd always wanted to try but never had the guts to. Hopefully, mastering a waltz or two might give her a quick-step in the right direction to boosting her self confidence.

Despite the digital maps clearly visible around the ship —for a brainiac she kept getting port and starboard mixed up—it took several attempts to find the ballroom. So much for her sure-fire navigational skills; apparently they only applied to the maze of one-way streets around Sydney and convoluted museum corridors.

Several women stood to one side of the ballroom while a few men loitered on the outskirts of the dance floor. She learned from Mavis, the woman standing next to her, that the men were hosts hired by the ship's company for single women who needed a dance partner.

"This is my seventh cruise, dear. Why do you think I keep coming back? Though I'm seventy, these dance hosts make me feel twenty-one again, whisking me all over the dance floor." Mavis winked. "Not to mention their youthful good looks."

Lana smothered a smile as the youngest host appeared to be a greying fifty-five. She observed the men skilled at mingling with the women and soon everyone had paired off. Predictably, she had no partner. Story of her life.

"Don't worry, love, you'll be the lucky one paired with the instructor." Mavis, the veteran cruiser, obviously knew how these things worked.

"I hope he's good."

Because she needed all the help she could get. Coordination and grace were not her strengths.

"I'm better than good. Let's just hope you can keep up."

Her nerve endings snapped to attention as the deep voice rippled over her and she didn't have to turn around to know who it belonged to. Fickle fate dealing her a bum hand yet again.

"Okay, class, let's get to work. As you can see, I'm not Rafe, our illustrious dance instructor. He was called away to a last minute rehearsal for tonight's extravaganza, so you're stuck with me instead. For those who don't know me, I'm Zac McCoy, the PR manager. Though I'm not a professional entertainer, I can safely say I don't have two left feet and I've managed to learn a thing or two during my years working with the entertainment staff. So, how about a waltz to start with?"

"Anything you want, handsome. Oh, if only I was thirty years younger." Mavis fanned her face, a twinkle in her eyes.

"If only I'd decided on taking the chess class," Lana muttered, wondering if she could fake a sprained ankle.

"Did you say something?" Zac's smug smile made her grit her teeth.

She had two choices. Duck and run as she usually would in an uncomfortable situation like this or ignore the blush burning her cheeks, ignore her qualms at never doing this before, suck it up, and see if she could get through this awkward encounter without making a fool of herself.

She shook her head, and managed a tight smile resembling a grimace. "No."

"Right then, shall we dance?"

Zac held out his hand, leaving her no option but to take it. She tried to relax, she really did, but as he pulled her closer, his body grazing hers, she inadvertently stiffened.

His knowing smile didn't help. "See, a perfect fit."

"I thought we were doing a waltz. The way you're holding me, seems more like the lambada."

"Fancy a bit of dirty dancing, do you?"

"Don't flatter yourself. You certainly don't hold a candle to Patrick Swayze."

A glint of hidden excitement lit his extraordinary eyes. "And here I was, thinking you were falling under my spell. You disappoint me."

She averted her gaze, focussing on anything other than those all-seeing eyes, wishing her heart would stop racing. "Don't you ever stop flirting?"

His grin widened. "I'm sure Fred did his fair share of flirting while he whisked Ginger around. I'm just taking my role seriously."

"Role as the resident Casanova you mean?"

The naughty glint in his eyes alerted her to the fact she hadn't insulted him. Moreover, he was enjoying their sparring way too much.

"We're both adults here. There's nothing wrong with a bit of harmless flirtation. Besides, you dared me, remember?"

More fool her. "Look, this is silly. You were taunting me last night, I bit back. Let's just forget it, okay?

The naughty glint didn't let up. If anything, it intensified as his lips kicked up into an all-too-sexy grin. "Unfortunately for you, I have a very good memory so I can't forget it. But I'm willing to concentrate on our dance steps for now?" and with that, he spun her outward at arms length.

"If that's your way of changing the subject, I'm not buying it."

He reeled her in with a slight tug on her hand. "Who said anything about needing to change the subject? I enjoy flirting, you're the one with the problem."

If he only knew.

She didn't know how to flirt, had zero experience. Jax had targeted her, played her, said all the right things, done all the right things to get her to fall for him. Flirting hadn't entered into it. As for her other two dates, they'd been stilted, awkward, rushed dinners with limited small talk and frequent glances at watches on both sides.

It wasn't so much as having a problem with flirting, she didn't have a clue how to do it.

She stumbled, winced, treaded on his toes, and wished the floor would open up and swallow her.

"Easy, Ginger. Just follow my lead."

If he'd smiled or smirked or had the faintest amused twinkle in his eyes she would've slammed her heel on his foot—well, thought about it—and made a run for it. Instead, he tightened his hold on her hand, gently increased the pressure with the other in the small of her back, and counted softly under his breath as he led her around the dance floor.

The counting was for her benefit but it didn't help. Clumsy, stiff, and awkward didn't begin to describe how she felt in his arms, like a mannequin given an airing before being dumped in a shopfront in only her knickers.

Thinking of knickers while in his arms had her trampling his toes again and she bit her lip, silently cursing her ineptness.

"Sorry." Her gaze fixed on his chest, heat scorching her cheeks.

He stopped twirling her about, placed a finger under her chin, and tilted it up so she had no option but to look at him.

"Don't apologize. This class is about learning and you're doing great for a beginner."

His understanding smile sent a tremor through her. Why couldn't he be condescending and obnoxious so she could dislike him, rather than considerate and kind?

She mumbled a noncommittal answer, wishing he'd stop staring at her like a pet project. Though it could be worse; he could've looked down on her as a charity case with pity in his eyes.

"Just feel the music. Let the beat take you."

Easy for Fred Astaire junior to say.

Her dubious expression had him chuckling as he pulled her closer again. "Come on, you'll enjoy it."

To her surprise, he was right. As soon as she stopped focusing on her feet not stomping his and ignored the fact he was holding her close, she started to relax. The music filtered over her, soft and ethereal, a classical hit from a bygone era, and she found herself humming softly, swept away in the magic of the moment.

She closed her eyes, remembering a dancing show she'd once seen on TV, and imagined herself in a siren red chiffon dress with a fitted bodice held up by willpower alone and handkerchief layers cascading from her waist to her ankles. She imagined snazzy red shoes to match, sequinned, with impossibly high heels that floated across the dance floor of their own volition.

With immaculate hair and makeup and the smile of a ballroom dancing champion, she lived the fantasy, let the music infuse her body, her senses, allowing Zac to whisk her around and around, her feet finally falling into step with his as an exhilaration she'd never known rushed through her.

She'd never felt so light, so graceful, so unselfconscious. If this is what ballroom dancing could do for her, she'd sign up for a year's worth of classes as soon as she got home.

But there was more to it than perfecting a waltz and she knew it. Zac had given her this gift, had given her the confidence to let go of her reservations and enjoy the moment. He'd empowered her to believe that for a precious few minutes she could be agile and lithe and elegant rather than a shy, clumsy klutz.

When the music faded, her eyelids fluttered open and rather than feeling let-down by reality, the gleam of appreciation in Zac's steady gaze had her craving to do it all again.

"You're good."

His admiration made her want to perform a few extra twirls for good measure.

She flushed with pleasure. "Thanks, so are you."

"You up for a cha-cha?"

Ignoring the usual flicker of nerves at trying something new, she nodded. "Sure. Let's give it a try."

Not only did she learn the cha-cha, Zac showed her the finer points of a foxtrot too. While the class danced around them, she matched him step for step, exhilarated by his fancy manoeuvres, thrilled by her increasing confidence to try more complicated steps.

At the end of an hour, she collapsed into a nearby chair, her face flushed, her feet aching, and her imagination still tripping the light fantastic.

He crouched next to her as she puffed at damp hair strands falling over her face, knowing she must look a hot, rumpled mess yet a small part of her feeling like that dance champion she'd imagined.

"You're full of surprises, aren't you?"

"Why? Because I only managed to break all the toes on your right foot and not your left?"

He laughed. "You'll be pleased to know my toes are fine. Better than fine, considering I had to do some fancy footwork out there to keep up with you once you got going."

There was a reason he was in PR. He probably laid it on this thick for countless other gullible females every cruise.

"Yeah, well, I told you I was good at the start." His eyebrows shot up, as he probably relived every clumsy stumble she'd made initially and she smiled. "And you're not such a bad teacher once you concentrate on the task at hand and tone down the charm."

"Thanks. I think." He stood, stretched, and she quickly averted her gaze from the sliver of tanned abs visible between his polo shirt and shorts. "See you tonight at dinner?"

His smile read pure invitation. If he'd asked her a few hours ago she would've sent him a short, sharp RSVP in the negative but after the enlivening hour she'd just spent thanks to him, she found herself nodding.

"Uh-huh."

"Right-o, see you then."

She fanned her cheeks as he walked away, wondering if it was the exercise, the exhilaration of feeling graceful for the first time in her life, or being wrapped in his muscular arms that made her hot and bothered.

In reality, she should be happy, ecstatic even. She'd tried something new today and had given her flagging confidence a much needed lift. Her sense of achievement was immense and she owed it to one guy.

After experiencing the rush of feeling graceful for the first time in her life, she wondered how much more he could boost her confidence if she didn't try so hard to fend him off?

## CHAPTER THREE

While Zac had impressed Lana with his sensitivity during dance class yesterday, he ruined it by slipping into full flirting mode over dinner last night. Her fledgling confidence hadn't lasted as she'd clammed up, grunted monosyllabic answers, and done her best to ignore the persistent attentions of a suave sailor with smooth moves and slick words.

She hated that it was a game to him because of a challenge she'd issued in a rash moment. Her inherent shyness was a bane she lived with every day; it affected her professionally, socially and romantically, yet he seemed to view it as something she could shrug off if he teased her enough.

He was really starting to get to her and thankfully, the ship had docked at Noumea today and she wouldn't waste another minute thinking about him. Instead, she explored the French-inspired capital of New Caledonia with its tree-lined boulevards flanked by trendy boutiques and cafés, enjoying every minute.

She savored the aroma of freshly brewed coffee mingling with tropical flowers, she scoffed melt-in-the-mouth flaky croissants, and she scoured the shops, something she never did back home. When she shopped it was for necessity rather than a burning need for retail therapy—no matter how many times Beth dragged her from one boutique to another trying to make her see otherwise.

Yet here, with the balmy breeze ruffling her ponytail and the tempting shopfronts laid out like sparkling jewels in the sun, she couldn't help but browse. Entering a small boutique, she meandered through the aisles crammed with clothes. Her hands drifted over soft silky sarongs and short strappy summer dresses before lingering over the swimwear. The only swimsuit she'd brought on this trip was an old black one piece cut high in the front, the one she used if she swam at home as part of a workout.

So why was she picking up a cerise bikini, the hot pink colour the exact shade her cheeks would be if she ever had the guts to wear something so revealing?

She put it down and eyed off some straw hats, before her gaze settled on the bikini again, drawn to it, mesmerised by its newness, its brightness, and its blinding contrast to everything she owned in her wardrobe.

Glancing down at her worn black flip-flops, khaki shorts, and well-washed grey T shirt, she hovered over the bikini, sorely tempted. Just looking at it gave her the same buzz she'd had when traipsing the dance floor in Zac's arms, the feeling she could be more assertive if she set her mind to it.

Spurred on by an eagerness to recreate that feeling, she snatched it up and headed for the counter before she changed her mind.

After thrusting the bikini at the young guy behind the counter, she ducked her head on the pretext of searching for her purse in her straw carry-all, hating how her cheeks burned when making a simple, everyday purchase for most women. She rummaged around, waiting for him to ring it up, unprepared for the small puff of perfume in the vicinity of her right ear.

"This fragrance will be perfect for mademoiselle."

She shook her head, ready to tell the sales assistant she wasn't interested, when an intoxicating blend of light floral tones mingling with subtle coconut drifted over her and she inhaled, savoring the heady scent, feeling surprisingly feminine with one small squirt.

She never wore perfume, had never owned a bottle in her life, but when the young guy stared at her with soulful, chocolate-brown eyes and insisted again it was perfect for her in a divine French accent, she found herself handing over her credit card and being handed back a duty free bag with two purchases she'd never dreamed of buying let alone using.

But for those few minutes when she'd watched him wrap the bikini and the perfume, she'd stood a little taller, felt a little braver, like she could be the type of woman who wasn't passed over for an amazing trip to Egypt as the museum's spokesperson just because she wasn't articulate or outgoing enough.

However, her flash of spirit didn't last as she strolled back to the ship, the perfume box banging against her leg, a constant reminder to its presence and she couldn't help but feel a fool. Since when did she wear perfume let alone go for something so...so...out there? *Sex on the Beach* was for girls not short on confidence, girls who'd have the guts to live up to the perfume's promise, girls who'd have the bravado to match wits with sailors relentless in their pursuit to prove a point.

Girls absolutely nothing like her.

Impulse buying a stupid perfume with a naughty name wouldn't give her the confidence boost she needed, nothing would, and she'd be better off remembering it rather than entertaining foolish dreams of showing everyone, Zac included, she wasn't the shy nerd they'd labeled her.

When she returned to the ship and her cabin, she flung the duty free bag into the wardrobe and slammed the door shut.

Regretting the waste of money—like she'd ever have the confidence to wear that bikini—she wriggled into her trusty one-piece and headed for the Dolphin deck pool. She dumped her towel on a deck chair before plunging into the water, eager to wash away memories of her recent foolishness. Closing her eyes she flipped over to float as a dark shadow passed over her. When it didn't move she opened her eyes.

And promptly sank.

Torn between the natural urge to fight her way to the surface for air or stay submerged, safely away from seductive sailors, she eventually floundered her way to the surface, spluttering and coughing.

"Need a hand?"

She glared at Zac's outstretched hand and shook her head, deriving small satisfaction as water droplets sprayed his immaculate uniform.

"No thanks."

His lips curved into a deliciously tempting smile. "You sure? I bet you'd be tempted to pull me in."

The thought hadn't crossed her mind but now he mentioned it, maybe a good dunking would cool him off... yeah, like she'd have the pluck to do that.

"Not really. And I'm quite capable of hoisting myself out of the pool if you'll move out of my way?"

"I like a strong woman."

She rolled her eyes. "You like women period."

"What's wrong with that? I'm a healthy red-blooded male."

Her gaze drifted across his broad shoulders of its own volition and lower, before snapping back to meet his all-too-confident stare. "I'll take your word for it."

She pushed away from the side of the pool, treading water, out of her depth physically and literally. Ever since she'd been silly enough to dare him that first night, he'd been teasing her, pushing her for a reaction. She wished she had the nerve to give him one.

"As much as I'm enjoying your mermaid impersonation, why don't you come a little closer so we can have a proper chat?"

"About?"

"Tonight. You and me."

How did he do that, infuse every word with mystery and mayhem and untold promise? As if his sexy smile and come-get-me eyes weren't enough.

For the second time in as many minutes she went under, cursing her inability to be anything other than be clumsy and inept in his presence. He unnerved her to the point of bumbling and it was high time she got over this funk he had her in with his constant teasing. Either that or jump ship.

She breast-stroked underwater to the side and hauled herself up the pool ladder. "Don't say a word. Just hand me that towel please."

He was smart as well as good-looking, for he didn't speak as he passed her the towel. Then again, he didn't need to. His smug smile said it all.

He had her squirming, wanting to match wits with him,

wishing she could yet scared of the consequences, her heart slamming against her ribcage at the thought of what they may entail.

For some strange reason he'd fixated his charm on her this cruise. Her, the last woman who'd reciprocate, the last woman to put up with his nonsense, the last woman to dally with if that was his intention. She wasn't a dallying type of girl, yet with him staring at her with a twinkle in those deep blue eyes it was hard not to wish she was.

"Aren't you at all interested to hear what I had in mind for you and me tonight?"

She was interested all right, interested to the point she'd almost drowned when he'd strung the words 'you and me and tonight' in the same sentence.

Tying the towel around her waist sarong-style, she aimed for casual. "I'm sure you'll tell me."

He chuckled. "Nice to see you this wound up. Must mean I'm getting somewhere in my quest to prove how much I like you."

"I'm not wound up."

She finished the knot at her waist with an extra hard yank, almost cutting off her circulation in the process.

"No?" He sent a pointed stare at the twisted mess she'd made of her towel and she stopped fiddling with it, crossing her arms instead.

Bad move, considering the wicked gleam in his eyes as he dragged them away from her cleavage.

"I just wanted to make sure you're coming to the island banquet. You won't want to miss it."

"That good, huh?"

"Better." His lowered tone indicated he wasn't just talking about the banquet.

This is where she struggled. She had no idea if he was

being clever or flirty or deliberately naughty, had no idea how to respond without sounding repressed and uptight or foolishly naïve.

"Well then, I look forward to seeing your prowess at organizing events."

"I'm sure you won't be disappointed with my *prowess*." He took a step toward her, ran his hand lightly down her arm, and she shivered, tiny goosebumps crawling across her skin as she belatedly realized she'd given him the upper hand yet again. "That's a promise."

Damn, he was good, too good. She should hoist the white flag now and surrender. He'd won. He'd bombarded her with enough smooth moves and clever words to prove he liked her. Though it was a game to him and she knew it.

Then why the urge to ignore her head, the logical part of her brain she always listened to, the part telling her to jump ship now before she was sucked into believing any of this was real?

"See you tonight." His husky tone washed over her like a warm wave, soft, soothing, seductive, as he grazed her arm in a fleeting touch before walking away, leaving her helpless and yearning and cursing her inexperience with men more than ever.

∽

Lana needed a shot of confidence and, in the absence of a ballroom dancing class, she settled for a squirt of that frivolous perfume she'd purchased in Noumea.

Considering her hand still shook as she pulled a brush through her hair, it hadn't work, and she contemplated staying in and ordering room service rather than face another inevitable encounter with Zac.

Her nerves were shredded. She couldn't pretend to be someone she wasn't and facing his incessant beguiling barrage would wear her down eventually and she couldn't handle that.

As she strolled towards the huge marquee about a mile from the ship where the banquet was being held, the warm trade winds ruffling the hair at the nape of her neck, she knew wearing a new perfume and hoping it would give her poise while under duress from Zac's charisma, was wishful thinking.

Fear settled in the pit of her stomach. Self-talk to stay cool and not let him rattle her was fine in the confines of her cabin, yet how would she stand up under pressure from his persistent charm?

Smoothing her old formal dress with nervous hands, she entered the marquee where suspended fairy lights created a magical effect as they reflected in the water. Tables lined the outskirts, heavily laden with local seafood delicacies, salads, and decadent desserts, and she tried not to drool. Easy, considering a persuasive sailor was nowhere in sight.

Mavis, resplendent in a vibrant teal floral dress and sporting an orange hibiscus tucked behind her right ear, sidled up to her, beaming as usual. "Aloha, dear."

Lana didn't have the heart to tell her the Hawaiian greeting wasn't used here. "You're looking very tropical."

"Yes, well, we've got to get into the island spirit, don't we? By the way, where's your beau? I haven't seen him."

"My beau?"

Mavis tut-tutted. "Don't play coy with me, my girl. I saw the way that sailor looked at you the other day in dance class. I may be old but I'm far from senile and if my eyes didn't deceive me, I think you liked the attention."

"No way—"

"Why don't you live a little and have some fun, dear? You're only young once." She snapped her fingers. "In order to do that you need to keep mingling and stop wasting your time talking to an old chook like me."

Mavis patted her cheek and said, "Say hello to that gorgeous sailor for me," and waddled away, chuckling under her breath

Lana wanted to have fun, she really did, but ignoring the habits of a lifetime was tough. Even if she knew how to flirt, would Zac be satisfied with that? She doubted it. If she responded, he'd take it as a signal she was interested in more, would probably expect more, and she couldn't give it to him.

She didn't do casual sex for a reason, a damn good one, and casting away her inhibitions along with her reservations would be impossible.

Unless she had great motivation?

Maybe she did, all wrapped up in six-foot-plus of sexy sailor?

Was Zac incentive enough for her to drop her guard and see where it led?

The thought had her bolting from the marquee for the safety of the deserted beach where she could quash daft thoughts like that before they blossomed and encouraged her to indulge in all kinds of crazy, uncharacteristic actions.

∽

Zac made small talk with a couple from Alabama while his gaze riveted to Lana as she left the marquee.

He was an expert at multi-tasking—his job, his *real* job, demanded it—so had no trouble nodding and laughing and responding to the couple while hiding a grimace at yet another hideous dress, this one in drab brown, and the way it hid Lana's curves.

And she had them, man, did she have them. He'd seen them on full display this afternoon despite that neck-to-knee ensemble—okay, it hadn't been that bad but those boring bathers were gruesome just the same—tantalizing curves that could give a guy ideas of how far he'd like to push this challenge despite every intention not to.

At least Lana had come. He'd had his doubts after the way he'd taunted her at the pool earlier. She was still nervous around him, something he couldn't figure out considering she'd come alive in his arms in that dance class after she'd loosened up, and the way she'd started smiling at some of his jokes over dinner.

Socializing didn't come naturally to her. He saw it in the fiddling fingers, the tense shoulders, the lowered gaze whenever his flirting got too heated. He should take pity on her and leave her alone.

An image of her in that wet, clinging, black one-piece sprang to mind again, instantly wiping his good intentions to keep his distance. The bathing suit hadn't been remotely sexy but the woman in it—now, that was another story.

All afternoon he'd mentally rehearsed the reasons he shouldn't push this thing between them: the 'employees don't fraternize with passengers' policy he'd devised himself, the importance of focusing on the quest to catch their spy, the debt he owed Uncle Jimmy. All perfectly legitimate reasons to keep his distance and stop toying with her.

But he couldn't get her out of his head. He'd never met anyone like her: fragile, shy, clumsy, yet infinitely endearing.

Simply, she captivated him.

It couldn't be purely physical, what with the old-fashioned clothes that hid her body rather than enhancing it. And she rarely wore makeup, tied her hair in a ponytail most of the time, and wore no jewellery.

But that was what intrigued him the most: her apparent lack of artifice allowing the natural intelligent sparkle of her expressive eyes to shine through, the genuine smile on the rare occasion one of his funny barbs struck home.

Her acerbic wit attracted him, the guarantee she wouldn't put up with any of his crap. He liked that, enough to know more, a lot more, and with curiosity egging him on, he bade goodbye to the couple and followed her.

The soft sand silenced his footsteps and he pulled up as Lana stopped at the ocean's edge, rubbing her arms before wrapping them around her middle, a vulnerable gesture that had him wondering who or what had put the wary expression in her eyes he'd glimpsed on more than one occasion.

For someone her age—he'd pegged as mid-to-late-twenties—she was too serious, too withdrawn, and each time he'd seen caution creep into her striking hazel eyes he wanted to slay whatever demon had put it there.

Crazy, considering his demon slaying days for any woman were long gone. Magda had seen to that.

Lana's posture screamed hands-off so what was he doing, disturbing her solitude? She wouldn't be up for another bout of flirting, another bout of teasing when he knew it couldn't lead anywhere. She'd made that clear.

He needed to leave her the hell alone, but before he took a step the breeze picked up and a waft of fragrance assailed his nostrils; he inhaled, savoring the tantalizing scent of frangipani with a hint of coconut. Pure ambrosia, piquant and addictive, and he shook his head to clear it.

He must've made a noise for she turned, pale moonlight casting alluring shadows over her face bathed in luminosity, her eyes wide and incandescent.

He'd never seen anything so stunning, the impact of her simple beauty hitting him like a blow to the solar plexus and, for an oxygen-starved moment, all he could do was stare.

"Sneaking up on me again?" The slight curve of her lips belied the hint of annoyance in her voice.

"You look like you could do with some company?"

"Maybe."

"You sure?"

"Don't sound so surprised. You're not too bad for a persistent pain in the butt."

He laughed, surprised she'd instigated a bit of light-hearted wordplay for the first time. "Be careful. That almost sounded like flattery and it might go straight to my head."

"Which part? The persistent pain part or the part where I actually admitted you're not too bad?"

"Take a guess."

She smiled. Breathtaking. "I'm sure you're well aware of your attributes, so anything I say isn't going to surprise you too much."

"My attributes, huh?" He flexed his biceps and squared his shoulders. "Nice to know you noticed."

She rolled her eyes. "See? I knew it'd go to your head."

He chuckled and closed the short distance between them, before ducking his head toward her neck. "What's that perfume, by the way? It's entrapment for any male that gets within five feet of you. Look at me; I'm putty in your hands at the moment."

"It's *Sex on the Beach*. Stupid name, but it smells okay. I bought it today in a fit of madness."

She stiffened imperceptibly at his nearness, meaning he should probably leave her alone.

But he couldn't.

Not when *Sex on the Beach* tripped from her lips like a saucy invitation, not when the words conjured up all sorts of wicked images in his over-heated imagination, not when she smelled and looked divine under a star-studded sky just made for romance and frivolity and getting swept away in the moment.

"Sex on the beach, huh?"

Her small nod brought her ear within nibbling range and he gritted his teeth, straightening, removing a delectable neck and ear out of temptations way, only to be confronted by a flicker of awareness warring with indecision in her unwavering stare.

"I couldn't resist it."

"Like I can't resist this." He lowered his lips toward her and her eyelids fluttered shut, a faint pink staining her cheeks, as their mouths finally fused.

He half-expected her to push him away but instead, her tentative acceptance of his kiss surprised him, pleased him, considering her usual reticence for anything beyond the mildest flirtation.

He'd wanted to do this for days, yet the anticipation of her lips touching his didn't compare to the reality.

As he rested his hands on her waist, spanning it, she combusted. There was no other description for her reaction as she wrapped her arms around him, tugging him closer, her hands frantic as they bunched his shirt, stroked his back, raking it while pushing against him, eager and spontaneous and incredibly responsive.

He deepened the kiss, demanding a compliance she was more than willing to give, her total abandonment firing his libido better than an aphrodisiac as she parted her lips, allowing his tongue to slide into her mouth where it wound around hers in an erotic, sensual dance he didn't want to end.

He groaned, threading his hands through her silky soft hair, loose and cascading over her shoulders for once, angling her head for better access to the warm delights of her mouth, wanting more, wanting it all.

He shouldn't be doing this. It defied logic, defied all reason, but her tongue touching his blasted every last shred of common sense out of his mind.

As her breasts pressed against his chest and her hands skimmed the waistband of his pants, sanity fled and he tore his mouth away, blazing a trail of hot, moist kisses down her throat.

Her head fell back, giving him full access to her neck and her deliciously delicate skin, so soft, so enticing, so tempting.

He couldn't get enough. He cupped her butt, pulling her against his arousal, wishing their damn clothes would disappear along with her inhibitions.

Lana gasped, her eyes flying open as the enormity of what they were doing felled her like a ten tonne anchor.

What the hell was she thinking?

Tolerating Zac's flirting was one thing, but this? This mind-blowing madness where she'd responded to him like a nympho?

The heat that had pooled in her belly crept upward, causing her neck to itch uncontrollably and her cheeks to light a beacon for the ship.

How could she have been so stupid? So wanton? So reckless?

She shoved her hair out of the way, dragged air into her lungs, and stepped away, desperate for physical distance, when a moment ago she'd been desperate for him.

His mouth kicked into a rueful smile. "I guess that perfume almost lived up to its name."

Soft moonlight reflected in his eyes and, while she couldn't fathom their expression, she knew hers must be horrified.

"Like hell." She blinked, wondering where that rapid retort had come from, the quick comeback almost shocking her as much as her eager response to his kiss.

To her amazement, he chuckled, a deep, rich sound that had no right warming her. "I suppose I should say this is my fault and that kiss was way out of line."

Her head snapped up, her stare accusing. "You're right on both counts, but you're not going to apologize, are you? You've been charming the pants off me ever since I issued that stupid dare, so the way your warped mind works, you probably think that kiss was inevitable."

"Charming the pants off you, huh?" He lowered his gaze to her dress and she blushed before jabbing a finger at him.

"You're incorrigible, you know that?"

"So I've been told."

He grasped her finger and lowered it, taking the opportunity to hold her hand, strumming the back of it with his thumb, soothing her anger when she was just getting worked up. Anger was good, anger was distracting, much better than focusing on the other emotions whirling through her: like wonder and awe and a soul-deep yearning to feel half as good now as she had for those brief seconds in his arms.

Zac eyeballed her. "What do you want to hear? That I've wanted to kiss you for days? Damn straight. Do I want a repeat? Hell yeah."

A few of Jax's parting shots echoed through her head: frigid, frosty, aloof, cold. How could she be any of those things when a kiss from Zac set her alight and he wanted a repeat performance?

But it couldn't happen again. Not when Jax's other parting comments still resonated: how their relationship had been a bit of fun, nothing serious, a fling. She'd given him her heart, he'd given her a case of male stage-fright for the next eighteen months and there was no way she'd ever get involved with a guy again without having the relationship parameters spelled out at the start.

As if a transient sailor who lived his life at sea would be interested in anything more than a fling.

She yanked her hand out of his and folded her arms. "A repeat is not an option." She frowned for good measure, her old prickly exterior firmly back in place. "It was a mistake. Just forget it."

He shook his head, the hint of a smile curving those incredible lips she'd never forget. "Impossible."

She had no idea if he was referring to not repeating the kiss or forgetting it, but no way was she asking for clarification.

With her head a riotous confusion of thoughts and her heart a frightening jumble of emotions, she knew she had to escape. Fast.

Her usual shyness wasn't justification for this desperate need to run. Uh-uh, this had more to do with the growing horror she'd totally embarrassed herself by kissing him like a sex-starved vixen and a deep, unshakeable fear she'd like to do it again.

"I have to go," she muttered, not waiting for a response as she kicked off her shoes, scooped them up with trembling hands, and dashed across the sand, wishing she could flee the memories of her insane response to his kiss as easily.

## CHAPTER
# FOUR

Lana tossed and turned all night, courtesy of a tall, handsome sailor with piercing blue eyes who commanded her dreams in explicit erotic detail.

Sleep-deprived and grumpy, she rolled out of bed at six, needing an aerobics class more than ever to work off some of her pent-up frustration. It worked at home when she had to unwind after dealing with missing freight or junior staff with non-existent people skills, so why not here?

Zac had kissed her.

And she'd responded, losing control for an insane moment in time, lowering her guard for a pair of persuasive blue eyes and a dashing smile.

She never allowed any guy to breach her defences, not since discovering Jax's deception and the aftermath, when he'd dumped her and trampled her hopes for a future in the process.

It was why she didn't indulge in fancy clothes or makeup or snazzy highlights in her hair. She was comfortable in her old skin, secure in using her bland appearance as a protective mechanism to ward off guys wanting more than she could give.

But Zac didn't seem to care. For some inexplicable reason, he saw past her dreary dresses and shabby chic, as if he saw the real her; a woman with needs, a woman who wanted to break free of her conservative mold but was too damn scared to try.

How ironic, that when he'd caught her off-guard with that kiss and she'd given in to temptation, her burgeoning confidence gained from the dance class and the perfume purchase retreated faster than a fleet under siege.

Now she had to deal with the aftermath of that scorching kiss and her cringe-worthy sex-starved reaction to ensure she forgot it and made damn sure it never happened again.

Once dressed, she headed for the gym. Exercising was familiar, cathartic, and would burn off the energy buzzing through her body since she'd lip-locked Zac. She needed to stop dwelling and replaying it in her head. It had happened, she couldn't take it back, so she needed to move on, protective armor firmly in place again.

Determined to stop brooding, she strode into the small gym crammed with about twenty ladies of varying shape, age, and attire, warming up on exercise bikes and treadmills. Some of her tension dissipated at the familiarity and she found a space, dropped her towel, and started stretching. She was midway through a hamstring stretch, her leg resting on a bar with her head almost touching her knee, when the instructor entered.

She froze, her hamstring giving a nasty twang as her leg slipped from the bar, when Zac strode past, barely breaking stride.

No way. Seeing him now was too soon, too awkward, too much.

He faced the room as twenty women sighed in unison. She didn't—she was supposed to be forgetting last night, remember—but she couldn't blame them, not with him standing there looking decidedly drool-worthy in navy shorts, white polo shirt, resident charming smile in place.

"Good morning, ladies. I can see you're all keen to start working out to be up this early. Unfortunately, Shelley had an accident ashore last night and has a severely sprained ankle. So I'm sorry, but these classes will be canceled for the remainder of the cruise."

Loud groans echoed through the room and Lana stifled a grin. Zac didn't have a clue how desperate a bunch of women craving their daily endorphin fix could be, and if he thought a simple apology would cut it, he was in for a big surprise.

"However, she'll be able to check your gym programs from tomorrow. She'll be here between ten and three, though purely in a supervisory role. Thanks for your understanding."

His thanks were pre-emptive. He'd barely finished speaking when angry women besieged him.

"You've got to be joking," said a thirty-year old in skintight black leggings and matching singlet. "I've saved for five years to take this cruise and that's it, no aerobic classes? I must do my classes every day."

"When I pay for service, I damn well expect it," said an octogenarian in a velvet leisure suit.

"The company who operates this ship will be hearing about this when I get off." This, from a fifty-something woman wearing serious workout gear.

"Isn't there anyone else to take over?" Asked the

youngest member of the crowd, a perky teen in a crop top and bike shorts.

Zac held up his hands, his smile long gone in the face of the tirade. "Ladies, please, if you'll give me a chance to—"

"Now listen here, mister. This is my tenth cruise and I've cruised with different shipping lines all over the world. So far, the service on this ship stinks." A large woman crow-barred into a purple leotard stood toe to toe with him, hands planted on ample hips. "Ever since I set foot on this tug, things have gone wrong. The air conditioning in my cabin didn't work, the balcony door jammed, the incompetent waiters mixed up my dinner, the dance instructor was called away at the last minute only to be replaced by the likes of *you,* and now this. What next?"

Another woman stepped forward, her rake-thin body clad in designer gear, the type you don't sweat in, and her artfully dyed blonde hair coifed for such an early hour of the morning.

"I'm surprised, Mr. McCoy. In my day, a PR man knew how to handle life's little dramas such as this. In fact, he was paid to promote the delights of cruising." Her eyes narrowed and her lips thinned in disapproval. "You, on the other hand, don't seem to be earning your wage at all. I would hazard to say you're rather incompetent."

Uh-oh. The situation had turned from tense to downright ugly in the space of two minutes and Lana felt sorry for Zac, wanting to help but unwilling to interfere.

Before Zac could utter a word, the designer dame jabbed an accusatory finger in his direction. "I presume you know who I am, Mr. McCoy?"

He nodded, his lips set in a grim line, but his confident aura firmly in place. She'd glimpsed the same unflappability last night after the kiss, when she'd slammed her barriers back in place and taken her anger out on him.

"Not only do Mr. Rock and I contribute handsomely to this particular shipping line, our personal recommendations go a long way to securing promotions for staff onboard. Personally, I'm having a hard time finding any worthy staff on this ship." She punctuated the air with short, sharp jabs of her hand. "And furthermore, I recommend you rectify this farce as soon as possible."

She spun around and sailed out of the room like the ocean liners of old, majestic, impressive, unstoppable.

Nobody deserved to be publicly berated like that and taking in Zac's tense posture and clenched jaw, Lana empathized. She knew what it was like to be on the receiving end of criticism like that, had faced it eight weeks earlier when she'd appealed to the museum's CEO to let her be the spokesperson on the Egypt trip.

The result? If her self-confidence hadn't been good to being with, it had been non-existent after that meeting when he'd told her in no uncertain terms she 'wasn't the face the museum was looking for'. Apparently, she was too reserved, too serious, too conservative. All perfectly legitimate qualities for head curator, but not good enough to front TV cameras and reporters at the digs of the newest discovery. That honor had gone to her trainee, a woman with a bigger mouth, bigger boobs, and a bigger wardrobe than her.

It had hurt. A lot. A whole damn lot. Lana was brilliant at her job, the one thing that made her feel good about herself. Little wonder her limited self-esteem had plummeted as a result and she needed this trip to give it a boost in the right direction.

Battling the sting of bitter tears and overwhelming

humiliation that day in the CEO's office, she'd pledged to gain confidence and never be overlooked for a work opportunity again.

After that kiss last night, she'd taken a huge backward step, retreat her best form of defence. But now, she possessed skills to help Zac, maybe she could take another baby step forward?

What better way than taking a class she'd been trained for?

She taught at the museum all the time, instructed students and peers, and it was the only time she never felt self-conscious in front of a group. She enjoyed teaching, enjoyed imparting skills to others, so why not here, now?

Clenching and unclenching her hands several times, she shook them out, wishing she could shake off her nerves as easily. Tension clawed at her tumbling tummy and she inhaled in and out, long, slow breaths to clear her head and give her clarity of thought.

But taking time to calm her nerves wasn't a good idea, as the more she thought about her proposition, the more she wanted to bolt for the safety of her cabin.

Though hiding away wouldn't improve her confidence.

It was now or never.

With a last deep indrawn breath, she marched toward Zac. "Could I have a word with you?"

As a low resentful grumbling resumed through the gym, he pinched the bridge of his nose, the first time he appeared rattled. "Now isn't the time."

"I can help. I'm a qualified fitness instructor. I can take this class right now if you want me to."

"You're a fitness instructor?" He made it sound like she was a space cadet as his assessing gaze swept over her.

Yeah, like her outfit made any difference to her credentials. "You really want to do this?"

"I wouldn't have offered otherwise."

Relief eased the tension in his face, as his lips kicked into a mischievous grin. "Does it mean I'll owe you?"

She almost ran at that point, the memory of that sexy smile seconds before he'd kissed her all too fresh as she focused on his lips.

"You won't owe me a thing."

"Oh, but I will."

Heck, how had this turned from her doing him a favor to having him in her debt?

With that beguiling smile and heat smouldering in his eyes, she was floundering out of her depth more than ever.

"Look, just forget it—"

"Go ahead and take the class but once you're done, drop by my office," he said, brusque and business-like, and she wondered if she'd imagined the loaded exchange a moment ago.

"Okay."

As she turned away, he laid a hand on her arm, her skin burning despite the innocuous touch.

"One more thing."

"What's that?"

"Just so you know, I always pay my debts." He paused, his disarming smile capable of tempting a saint. "And I fully intend on doing that with you."

His eyes glittered with intent before he released her and walked away.

∽

Lana tucked strands of frizz into her bristling ponytail, all too aware she was fighting a losing battle as she stared at her flushed face covered in perspiration sheen. The polished brass nameplate on the door to Zac's office was highly effective as a mirror, too effective as she belatedly realized she should've ducked down to her cabin before presenting here.

When he'd said he'd see her after class he wouldn't have anticipated a bedraggled, scraggly mess lobbing into his office. Then again, it wasn't like she was trying to impress him. The opposite, in fact. The sooner he realized he couldn't charm her like every other woman on the planet, the easier her life would be, even if a small part of her would miss his banter.

She knocked and waited for a 'come in' before pushing the door open, the sight that greeted her snatching the breath from her lungs.

She'd seen his many facets: sailor Zac resplendent in uniform, dancing Zac, dinner companion Zac, yet the sight of him behind a desk, pen scrawling across a daily planner in one hand, fingers flying across a keyboard with the other while issuing instructions into a phone, had her grabbing the door to steady her wobbly knees.

Zac made multi-tasking look easy, a guy in total control who could do anything he set his mind to, and when he glanced up and smiled in welcome she had to steel her resolve, for executive Zac was as appealing as the rest of his personas. More so, considering she understood business, thrived on business, her life was all business.

"I'll get back to you. In the meantime, make sure those timetables are correct to within a second." He stabbed at the disconnect button on the phone, threw his pen down, and leaned back in his chair, hands clasped behind his head. "Well, well, if it isn't our very own aerobics instructor."

With a shrug, she crossed the room and sat into a chair opposite him. "You make it sound like I don't know what I'm doing."

"Sorry, you surprised me, that's all. How did it go? Bet those women didn't give you a hard time."

"Why would they? I'm good at what I do. Besides, I think they took out all their frustrations on you."

"Did they ever." He lowered his hands and stood, his sudden proximity making her rethink her choice of seat. The wide, stuffy leather chair in front of his desk had seemed perfect while he was seated but now, with him towering over her, it wasn't so good.

"Thanks for stepping in and saving my butt."

Oh no. She wouldn't think about his butt...wouldn't go there...wouldn't remember how she'd made a grab for it last night in that fit of insanity.

Grateful she could blame her flaming cheeks on exercise rather than embarrassment, she cleared her throat. "You're welcome."

"Now that you're here, it's time we had a chat."

"About?"

His eyes bored into hers, challenging, determined, as he gestured toward a document on his desk.

"Your employment contract, of course."

## CHAPTER
# FIVE

"Pardon?"

Lana tapped her ears, just to make sure she'd heard correctly.

He picked up the document and offered it to her. "Take a look. It's your employment contract."

"You're kidding, right?" She stared at the document like it was her marching orders to walk the plank. "I'm on vacation. A well-earned vacation, I might add. I helped you out of a tight spot back there in the gym, but that's it."

He threw the contract on a pile of folders and perched on the desk in front of her, way too close for comfort. "I understand how you feel, but I need your help. You'd only have to take two classes a day. In return, you'll be well paid and it won't interfere with your vacation. You love your job, don't you?"

"My job?"

A puzzled frown knit his brow. "You said you're a qualified fitness instructor?"

"I am."

But that wasn't her job. Her job entailed wearing boring

business suits, cataloguing boring artefacts, and devising boring staff rosters.

Okay, so she loved her job, and it wasn't always dull, but after she'd been passed over for the Egypt trip she'd started craving more, and strangely, the opportunity now came from the most unlikely source as she stared at him.

In that moment, it hit her like a meteor from Mars.

She needed to build her confidence this trip, wanted to try new things, but still felt stifled by her conservative nature. What if she stepped into a new role? Became the type of person she'd like to be if she had more nerve?

Besides, she wasn't lying. She *was* a qualified aerobics instructor, she just didn't do it for a living.

And who knew, maybe doing this would give her the tenacity to form a coherent answer without wanting to duck her head in embarrassment every time Zac smiled her way?

"Let me take a look at that."

Trying to hide a triumphant grin and failing, he handed her the contract. "I took the liberty of contacting Madigan Shipping, the company that owns the Ocean Queen. I explained the circumstances and they approved a temporary employment contract, particularly when they heard the Rocks were onboard. They're influential people in shipping circles."

"Do you always organize other people's lives or will I actually have a say in your grand plan?"

His grin broadened. "You're here, aren't you? And I'm giving you the option to sign on or not."

"Yeah, right."

Skimming the contract, Lana nearly fainted when she spied the remuneration, on par with her monthly salary. For taking two classes a day? Too easy. And she had been coveting a new futon for the spare bedroom in her flat. Not to mention the slight shoe fetish she'd developed thanks to Beth's cast-offs, and this extra cash would come in mighty handy for a pair or two of her own.

"What do you think?"

"I think I'm nuts, but what the heck." She picked up the pen he'd discarded earlier and signed the contract. "There."

"Don't forget, I owe you." His eyes glowed, magnetic and enticing, and she suppressed a shiver of longing at what his payment might entail.

"Don't worry about it." She tugged at her ponytail, twisting the ends around her finger in a nervous habit she'd had since childhood. "This is turning into some vacation. The ship's amazing, the ports are interesting, then that kiss last night—"

She bit her tongue and mentally slapped herself for running off at the mouth and thinking out loud. That kiss was history, remember? Forgotten.

His gaze riveted to her mouth, her lips tingling as his blistering stare focused, and she surreptitiously itched behind her ear where her skin prickled the most.

What had happened to the woman who'd just instructed an aerobics class for the first time and nailed it? What happened to her newfound bravado? Looks like it had deserted her, along with her common sense, for thinking she could sign on as an employee and keep her distance from Zac.

She fidgeted, shifting weight from one foot to the other, rubbed the nape of her neck, wound hair around her finger again, and his gaze finally lifted from her mouth only to lock onto her eyes, all that endless blue enticing and intense.

She looked away first and gestured to the desk. "Don't you have work to do?"

"It can wait."

She couldn't stand the tension, the air practically crackling between them, and she backed toward the door. "Well, I need a shower so I better go."

He stalked toward her, like a powerful alpha wolf shadowing a helpless, quivering rabbit.

"But what about figuring out what I owe you?"

She waved her hand, fluttering, ineffectual at keeping him at bay. "The payment's all there in the contract. Clearly spelled out in black and white."

He stopped less than a foot in front of her and leaned forward. "Nothing's ever that clear. There are many shades of grey here that I think we need to figure out."

Her breath caught as his head lowered, her heart pounding like she'd just taken ten aerobic classes back to back.

"Like?"

It came out a squeak and she darted a glance to the door handle a few inches from her hand. She should grab it, twist it, and make a run for it, but she couldn't, trapped beneath that disconcerting stare, overpowered by his sheer masculinity as he towered over her.

For one insane second she almost wished he'd kiss her again and get it over with but instead, he straightened, ran a hand through his hair and pointed at his desk.

"Like a stack of paperwork, tax forms and the like that you need to fill out. How about you go take that shower and meet me back here in half an hour?"

She almost collapsed against the door in relief—or was that disappointment?

Buoyed that she'd had a lucky escape, she saluted. "Aye, aye, sir."

With her hand on the door handle, she couldn't resist the parting shot considering he'd had the upper hand ever since she'd set foot in here. "You know something? I'm looking forward to being your colleague. You might actually let up on me if we're co-workers."

After Lana closed the door, Zac sank into his chair and stared at the contract she'd signed, the fine print blurring.

Colleague.

Co-worker.

Lana Walker, the woman who was slowly but surely driving him crazy, was now a colleague, neatly circumventing his golden rule of never getting involved with a passenger.

Hell.

He leaned back and closed his eyes. It didn't help, as an image of pert breasts, narrow waist, toned abs, and slim legs covered in lycra haunted him. She wasn't tall, yet her perfect proportions gave the illusion of height, and he ached to touch her, every tempting inch.

Damn it, why couldn't she stay hidden behind those loose dresses and revolting pants she wore? First the wet one-piece and now this: tight candy-striped lycra bike shorts and a white T-shirt, fitted enough to highlight the curves he'd love to run his hands over.

He'd snuck back to the gym to watch the last few minutes of her class and had been blown away.

In a whirl of high kicks and arm twirls and jiggling breasts, Lana had morphed from shy innocent to sex goddess, and no matter how hard he tried he couldn't wipe her from his mind.

This teasing was getting out of hand. It had been fun at

the start, amusing to get a smile from that prim mouth, a rare fiery flash in those somber hazel eyes. But somewhere along the way the lines had blurred, and what had started out as a bit of harmless fun to get a subdued woman to lighten up had morphed into him wanting her. Seriously wanting her, his thoughts consumed by her, day and night.

That kiss on the beach last night had changed everything.

He'd given in to temptation, unprepared for the ferocity of her response, a response that had kept him up all night wishing he hadn't let her flee. If her enthusiasm last night hadn't captivated him enough, her metamorphosis from shy and nervous to bouncy and brilliant in that exercise class had him wondering what else she was hiding beneath her prim and proper facade.

She intrigued him, and despite the importance of keeping his mind on the job this cruise, he had to know more.

What was it about her that had him coiled tighter than an anchor chain?

He rubbed his temples, but it did little to erase the beginnings of a headache building behind his eyes.

Forthright and tetchy Lana was not his type at all, yet she was so delightfully unaffected, with an underlying hint of vulnerability that tugged at his heartstrings no matter how hard he tried to ignore the fact he still had a functioning heart.

But he couldn't get involved; at least not emotionally. He had his reasons. Besides, how would she feel if she knew he'd conned her?

He didn't place that ship-to-shore call. He didn't have to.

One of the perks of being the boss, even if no-one knew it yet.

Being the boss meant he needed to get back to work. He was so close to discovering the leak that was threatening to drown the company. His uncle's suspicions had been well-founded and the sooner he found the mole who hadn't disclosed corporate espionage as a skill on their CV, and saved the company a few billion dollars give or take, the easier things would be for his uncle.

He owed Jimmy and like he'd promised Lana, he always paid his debts.

So what would she think of the purely carnal payback system he'd like to instigate with her?

∽

LANA STOOD UNDER THE SHOWER, cool water sluicing down her body. She closed her eyes and tilted her head back, enjoying the spray peppering her face, though it did little to wash away the memory of that damn kiss.

She was determined to forget it, to relegate it to the back of her mind alongside other recoil moments, like walking in on one of her students with the museum taxidermist in a decidedly unstuffy moment in the archive room, and bawling when she'd got her first promotion.

Truly shuddery, cringe-worthy moments, just like her response to that kiss last night.

Then why couldn't she wipe the memory however hard she tried?

After turning off the taps and stepping out of the shower, she dried off, then tipped her head forward and tied the towel turban-style around her dripping hair. When she straightened, a few spots danced before her eyes, along with a vision of Zac's hungry stare as she'd left his office. She could blame the blood rushing to her head as she'd bent over, then draining as she straightened too fast, but she knew the truth.

The guy was unforgettable, every infuriating inch of him.

Not that she'd wanted to provoke him, far from it. He delighted in rattling her, in teasing her, and she'd wanted to fire a barb back. But it hadn't worked. The desire in his gaze had been real, potent and oh-so-scary for a novice like her.

Old Lana would've jumped ship and swum back to shore before he could wink. But she wasn't the old Lana anymore.

The old Lana wanted a husband, a family, a house in the suburbs to come home to every night after another satisfying day at the museum.

The new Lana still wanted all those things, but for the first time in her life she was experiencing the flicker of excitement that came with self-assurance, the heady rush of having a guy like Zac pay attention to a geek like her.

She'd never had that. Jax had faked a few compliments, fuelled her need to be noticed by a guy, any guy, and reeled her in as part of his plan. He'd used her before saying she was frigid when she couldn't deliver what he'd wanted. His disdain haunted her to this day.

She knew his accusation was why she didn't date very often, why she froze when a guy got physically close.

So why had she combusted in Zac's arms during that kiss?

Subconsciously, she knew. She wanted to feel alive, wanted to tap into the passion simmering deep inside, wanted to be bold and brazen and beautiful rather than a mousy, mundane workaholic.

Zac had a way of looking at her, as if she was the only woman in the world, and when he did, the small, wistful part of her that wanted to be that confident woman dared to hope.

∼

Lana made it back to his office with a minute to spare.

"Come on in. I've got the forms for you."

"Great."

As she stepped into the office, he briefly touched her elbow, bending lower on the pretext of closing the door. "What, no perfume?"

Her gaze snapped to his, only to catch a fleeting glimpse of a cheeky grin before he turned away, her scowl wasted.

"Why don't I take them away with me, fill them out, and drop them at the front desk when I'm done?"

She may be feeling braver after breezing through the class but there was something about him now, the way he looked at her, as if seeing her in a new light. While she should be happy, her inner introvert trembled at what he might do if he sensed the change in her.

He tapped the stack on his desk and beckoned her over. "Believe me, when you take a look at these you'll be thanking me for filling them out here. I've helped employees through the rigmarole before, we'll get it done in half the time."

Okay, so he was being helpful. Then why did it feel like he was toying with her?

"Right, let's get to work then." She sat on the chair opposite his and drew the forms toward her.

He stilled her hand by placing his on top, setting her pulse racing as she stifled the urge to yank hers away. "Not much intimidates you, does it?"

She raised an eyebrow. If he had any idea how her heart thumped, her lungs seized, and her insides quaked at his simple touch, he'd withdraw that statement.

"I can usually handle stuff."

Professionally, that is. Anything else and she was as poised as a toddler on ice-skates.

"Think you can handle me?"

His voice had dropped seductively low, the smouldering flame in his eyes warming her, warning her that she was in way over her head if she thought for one second a small boost in confidence could cope with Zac at his tempting best.

"I'm sure it wouldn't be too hard."

She almost bit her tongue in frustration, unwittingly adding to the wordplay as heat suffused her cheeks, wishing she had the spunk to toss her hair over her shoulder not duck her head like the blushing virgin she almost was.

His grin had tension strumming her taut muscles. "You're very assured when you want to be."

Using her brain to fend off his quick retorts, maybe. Easier than admitting she was lousy socially.

"Mainly when putting guys like you back in your place."

He leaned forward, close enough to whisper in her ear. "Guys like me?"

Resisting the urge to jerk back from his proximity, she settled for a subtle slide of her hand out from under his instead.

"Overconfident. Smooth. Charming. Used to getting your own way."

Rather than being offended, he laughed. "Guilty as charged."

He leaned into her personal space again, crowding her, overwhelming her, confusing her. "So is it working?"

"What?"

"My charm."

"Not a bit." She crossed her fingers behind her back for the little white lie. "Now, if there's nothing else, let's get these forms done so I can enjoy my vacation."

"Actually, there was something else. You know I owe you?"

"Uh-huh."

The instant wariness in Lana's eyes made Zac chuckle.

"How about a tour when we dock in Suva? I've got the day off so could show you the sights. What do you think?"

Her eyes lost their cautious edge as her lips curved into a smile, the type of genuinely happy smile that could easily tempt a man to want more, a lot more.

"Sounds good. Know any hot spots?"

Yeah, just below her ear, above her collarbone, and dead-on her soft lips.

"Several."

His tone must've alerted her to his thoughts for her eyes widened and glowed with understanding, until he could distinguish the tiniest green flecks in the molten caramel before the shutters quickly descended.

"The tour sounds great." She lowered her gaze in record time, her tongue darting out to moisten her top lip, the nervous action doing little to dissipate his growing interest in discovering what really made this enigmatic woman tick.

Considering how much he wanted to get to know her, perhaps he should rethink Suva, especially the part about taking her to his favorite secluded beach. If he could barely keep his hands off her here, what hope did he have in blissful isolation on the most spectacular stretch of pristine sand he'd ever seen?

"Right, it's a plan."

He'd almost said date, but dates implied more of that physical stuff he was trying to ignore. No matter how hard he tried, he couldn't wipe the vivid fantasy of the two of them splashing in the lagoon, him play-wrestling her, her wrapping her legs around him, wet skin plastered to his, no clothes...

She stood abruptly, the chair almost toppling. "Look, I really appreciate the offer to help but I'll be fine with these forms. I'll holler if I need to."

By her shaky voice, she knew exactly what he was thinking and reacted how she usually did: by erecting verbal barriers or making a run for it.

She scooped up the papers and made a dash for the door in a fluorescent flurry of a floral ankle-length skirt the color of a lifejacket, her hurried departure leaving him shaking his head as she slammed the door.

After she left, he sank into his chair and swiped a hand over his face. It didn't help. He could still see her wide-eyed guarded expression, the hint of suspicion in those hazel depths, the cynical curve of her lips.

She didn't trust him, didn't accept his interest as real. Not that he blamed her. He'd given her no indication to the contrary, playing the flirt, keeping things light-hearted, seeing how far he could push her before she reacted.

Either someone or something had made her into a sceptic and he'd hazard a guess some jerk had done a number on her. It would explain her naivety and lack of artifice when it came to playing coy or flirting. Which meant he should give her a wide berth. Instead, he wanted her with a staggering fierceness, the depth of his need obliterating every common sense reason why he shouldn't do this.

He didn't need the distraction. He had a job to do. But if his head kept spinning like a compass needle his concentration would be shot anyway, so maybe he should spend some time getting to know her, the real her, not the cagey woman who hid her mistrust behind lowered eyes and fiddling hands.

Muttering a few curses which wouldn't make many of his colleagues blush, he picked up the phone and placed his daily call to Jimmy.

The phone rang three times precisely, the same number every day, which proved his uncle waited by the phone despite protests to the contrary that he trusted him and the company was in safe hands.

When Jimmy picked up, Zac said, "Hey Uncle, it's me."

"Zachary, my boy. How's things?"

Where should he start? The part where he still felt like a fraud running the company from behind the scenes until their culprit was caught or the part where he was crazy for a woman who bolted every time he got close?

"Fine. I'm making progress."

He didn't need to spell it out. His uncle had been the first to notice their profit margins slipping, the first to see their biggest rival undercutting costs and getting better deals from suppliers.

And though Jimmy would never admit it, the ensuing stress hadn't helped his battle with the illness that was slowly but surely killing him.

"Good. Because once you sort out the Australian side of things, there's that Mediterranean problem that needs attention."

"All under control."

Zac had signed on for the European run for a year, more to do with the old man needing him rather than business. Not that Jimmy wanted to be mollycoddled. He'd made that perfectly clear, but under all that gruffness was a scared man fighting to stay alive and Zac would be damned if he left the only father he'd ever known alone at a time like this.

He wanted to ask how he was feeling, how the treatment was going, knowing he'd get the usual brush off.

"So how are things in London?"

"All good here."

He heard the strain beneath the forced upbeat tone.

"And you? How are you feeling?"

A slight pause followed by a grim throat clearing. "Can't complain."

James Madigan wouldn't. He hadn't complained when Zac had left him in the lurch for a year when he'd run off to marry Magda, he hadn't complained when he'd had a near fatal heart attack as a result of the ensuing stress from an increased workload—picking up the slack because of *his* selfishness—hadn't complained when Zac had outlined his plans for the future in direct opposition to his.

Jimmy was that sort of man: rock-solid, steadfast, a man Zac owed everything to, a man he aspired to be.

"The PR stint working out okay?"

"Yeah, the staff's buying it and I'm getting the info I need so that's the main thing."

Jimmy coughed, an ear-splitting hacking cough that chilled Zac's blood.

Aware his uncle hated appearing weak in the slightest he quickly tried to distract him. "Get this. I had Helena Rock on my case this morning, going berserk. Can't tell you how close I was to telling her I actually run the company now. That would've put the battle-axe back in her place."

Jimmy chuckled, something he wished he could hear more often. "Lucky you didn't, otherwise you'd have a mutiny on your hands. Imagine if everyone knew I'd made you head honcho and hadn't announced it officially yet? You wouldn't get the info we need to nail the bastard bleeding us dry."

"You're right, but I hate lying. The staff respects and trusts me as a fellow employee. I feel like I'm using them."

"Don't be ridiculous, this is business. Cruise lines are becoming more competitive every day so why shouldn't we use a bit of know-how to get ahead? It's your company now." Jimmy paused, the rattle in his throat indicating another cough coming on. "I'd do the same if I could. Unfortunately, I'm just an old sea dog who has to live vicariously through you these days, so make sure you do a damn good job."

Zac searched for the words to reassure his uncle, to try to explain he couldn't be prouder of the responsibility he'd been handed despite the doubts crawling into his subconscious at the oddest of times and making him feel a fraud.

"I wouldn't have placed you in charge of this empire unless I thought you were capable, Zachary."

As if reading his mind, Jimmy knew the right thing to say at the right time, as usual.

"Yeah, a regular shipping magnate, that's me."

He'd wondered why his uncle had pushed him into shipping after he finished his commerce degree, not twigging that the crafty codger was grooming him until a year into his first contract. By then Zac had been hooked, addicted to a shifting deck under his feet and the tang of salt air in his lungs.

## THE CEO

He was proud to be in charge of the Madigan Shipping Conglomerate and would do whatever it took to make it the best shipping line in the world. He had big boat shoes to fill. He owed Jimmy. Now, more than ever.

"You're doing a fine job, my boy. Now, you better get back to work. Just because you're the boss doesn't mean you can slack off."

Zac laughed, half raising his hand in a salute, like he used to when he was a little boy, before dropping it uselessly, all too aware he wouldn't have much time left to share a joke with his uncle.

"You look after yourself."

He only just heard a mumbled "You're as bad as these damn nurses," before Jimmy hung up.

Life was short. Seeing a strong, vibrant man like Jimmy fade away reinforced that and Zac would be damned if he sat here and let Lana disembark next week without fully exploring this unrelenting attraction driving him to seek her out almost every second of the day.

He didn't want to look back on this time and regret it, didn't want to be left with memories of a kiss and little else.

She could run but she couldn't hide and tonight, he'd make sure she knew exactly how much he wanted her.

A woman like Lana needed to be wooed, deserved to be treated right, starting with a romantic first date designed to bring a smile to her face and banish her doubts he was anything other than genuine—in his pursuit of her, at least.

# CHAPTER
# SIX

Against her better judgment, Lana had fallen under Zac's spell.

He'd flirted with her all through dinner, flattering her, teasing her, making her laugh. By the time she finished a divine lime tart smothered in lashings of double cream, her sides and her cheeks ached from smiling, and he'd well and truly slipped under her guard despite logic telling her he was playing a game.

"Fancy having a coffee in one of the lounges?" He leaned toward her, immediately creating an intimacy that set her pulse racing, throwing her off balance quicker than the two metre swells buffeting the ship.

"Only if you ease up with the compliments."

"Why?" His eyes darkened like storm clouds scudding across a midnight sky.

"It's overkill."

"But all true."

She raised an eyebrow and sent a pointed look at her unadorned navy shift dress. "You think I look good in this?"

His gaze dipped to her dress, then lifted to focus on her

lips, before his curved into a roguish smile. "What you wear is irrelevant. You're beautiful."

She exhaled on a soft sigh, wishing for one incredible moment she could be seduced into believing him by his low voice, his hypnotic eyes, his sincere expression. But she wasn't beautiful, far from it, and falling under a suave sailor's spell was beyond foolish.

"Now that you've exercised your smooth lines for the evening, maybe I will have that coffee. I'm in need of a caffeine hit to wake me from the stupor you've got me in after all that BS you're shovelling."

He laughed. "It's a date. Just let me drop by the office to check on a fax and I'll meet you in the Crow's Nest Lounge in ten minutes?"

"Make it five."

"Can't bear to be away from me for long?"

"Actually, I was thinking more of the fact that I need to be up early for my first official aerobics class so don't want to be out too late."

"Spoil sport. I thought you might be pumping up my ego for a delusional moment there."

"Like you need it." Tapping her watch face, she shot him a saccharine-sweet smile. "Four minutes and counting. If you want that coffee you better get a move on."

He held up three fingers. "Bet I beat you there."

"You're on."

She made a dash for the bathroom on the way, unable to resist touching up her lipstick. Woeful behavior for a girl who rarely wore anything but a slick of gloss back home, but considering Zac kept studying her like she was a priceless painting she had no choice. That sort of scrutiny put a girl under pressure, especially one who didn't feel beautiful let alone believed she deserved compliments, and she needed all the help she could get.

As she strolled into the Crow's Nest with ten seconds to spare, her stomach somersaulted as she caught sight of Zac at a cozy table for two in the farthest corner, beckoning her over with a smug smile.

"What did you do? Sprint the whole way?"

He pulled out a seat for her and she sank into it before her knees gave their telltale wobble whenever he got too close.

"I ducked into the office and the fax hadn't arrived, so I headed straight here. What about you? Have a quick dip overboard before you joined me?"

She tilted her nose in the air, her stare withering as she feigned indignation. "First I'm beautiful, now I look like a drowned rat. You need to work on your charm."

"That's what you're here for." He trailed a fingertip down her forearm and her breath caught. "I need the practice. Now, fancy a coffee? A drink?"

"Make mine a double," she muttered, snatching her arm away, her disapproving glare doing little to curb his sexy smile.

"Really?"

She waved him away. "No, just order me something sweet and yummy."

"You've already got it, but I'll get you a drink too."

Poking her tongue out in response to his corny comeback, she waited until he headed to the bar before grabbing a coaster and fanning her face.

Every second she spent in Zac's charming company confused her further, but she'd agreed to his invitation because she didn't want to head back to her tiny cabin just yet.

Tonight was the anniversary of Jax spitting the truth at her, the night he'd dumped her in no uncertain terms. While she'd made a new life, moved to a new city, taken up new activities, she couldn't forget the devastation and embarrassment after making such a monumental error in judgment in allowing him into her heart.

She couldn't be alone tonight. She needed to be distracted with funny quips and compliments no matter how meaningless, a night to erase the memories of how naïve she'd once been.

"Are you okay?" Zac asked, as he placed their drinks on the table and pulled his chair closer to hers, concern creasing his brow.

Annoyed that how morose she'd been feeling must've shown on her face for a moment, she blinked rapidly and pointed to her contact lens. "Still not used to these darn things. Spectacles are so much easier."

His eyes narrowed as they locked onto hers, probing yet compassionate. "I'd believe you if I hadn't seen your expression."

He jerked his thumb over his shoulder toward the bar. "From over there, you looked like someone had died. Then I get back here and you're almost crying—"

"I'm not." She sniffed as a lone tear chose that moment to squeeze out of her eye and roll down her cheek, plopping on the back of her hand clenched in her lap.

"The hell you're not." He brushed a thumb under her eye, so tenderly she almost burst into tears on the spot. "Why don't you tell me what's really going on?"

She shook her head, mortified he'd seen her like this, frantically wracking her brain for something halfway plausible to tell him, anything other than the truth.

He placed his hand over hers, and gave an encouraging squeeze. "Tell me."

She opened her mouth, closed it, and repeated her goldfish impersonation, her mind blank apart from the glaring truth: that it had been eighteen months since Jax dumped her and the memory still had the power to make her blubber.

"It's a guy, isn't it?" His mouth settled into a grim line. "What did the jerk do?"

Her gaze focussed on his, her tears rapidly drying under all that fierce, fiery blue. He almost looked possessive, protective, and she found herself wanting to tell him, a small part of her thrilled he actually seemed to care.

"Tonight's an anniversary of sorts." She stared down at his hand covering hers: tanned, comforting, strong. Some of that strength transferred to her as she took a deep breath and exhaled slowly. "I loved this guy, thought he was the one. He said all the right things, did all the right things, but turned out he was only after one thing."

She almost blurted the truth, that Jax had only been schmoozing her for what she could do for him at the museum. He'd wanted insider info on items for his private collection, but Zac couldn't know about any of that, considering he thought she was a fitness instructor.

Not that it would matter if she told him the truth about her real job, but she'd caught him watching her conduct that aerobics class when she stepped in to save his butt, and she'd never had any guy look at her like that: with intense need, like he couldn't look away.

She liked how it made her feel—empowered that she could make a guy like him want her—and telling him she was a museum curator now would be irrelevant anyway.

"We didn't really click, so he dumped me." She

shrugged, hating the lance of pain still lodged deep in her heart. "He said I was just a fling, a bit of fun."

She hiccupped, a pathetic half-sob, angry at the sting of tears, furious for being such a gullible fool. "He laughed at me for getting so involved, for being 'old-fashioned' in taking our relationship seriously."

Zac cursed under his breath and turned his hand over to intertwine his fingers with hers. "You listen to me. That piece of slime didn't deserve you. He isn't worth anything, let alone you giving him a second thought."

"I know." She sighed, enjoying the secure feeling of her fingers intertwined with his way too much. Holding her hand was a fleeting, comforting gesture, something a guy like him would do. But for one, tiny moment, it made her feel beyond special, like he really cared.

"Come with me." He leaped to his feet, practically dragging her with him.

"But what about our drinks?"

"Forget them. Let's go."

"Where?" She had to almost run to keep up with him, his long strides determined.

"Somewhere I should've taken you first rather than easing into this date with a drink."

Her jaw hit the deck as he pushed through a heavy glass door and led her out onto the open promenade. "Date?"

"Yeah, date. You know, that thing two people do when they want to get to know each other better, when they like each other, even if one of them doesn't want to admit it."

If her mind spun with memories of Jax, it positively reeled now with Zac's little announcement.

They reached the railing and he finally released her hand and leaned forward, his gaze fixed on the undulating ocean. "I've gone about this all wrong. I didn't want to scare you off by calling this a date tonight, but I'd planned on bringing you up here, talking a little, getting to know each other, before catching a movie or maybe going dancing, or whatever you wanted to do."

She couldn't speak, the pain of Jax's memory annihilated by the unbelievable joy unfurling in her heart.

He turned to face her, reaching up to stroke her cheek with his thumb, as she held her breath, stunned by his intimate touch and her craving for more.

"I wanted tonight to be romantic, to show you I'm not just toying with you." He stepped closer, took hold of her arms, and she stifled a gasp, captivated by the moonlight glinting off his dark curls and the striking shadows it created as it played across his face. "What do you think? Care to date a sailor with more than flirting on his mind?"

He slid his hands up and down her arms, the rhythmic contact depriving her of all rational thought as he gazed at her with hunger and greed and passion.

"I don't know what to say—"

"Then don't say anything at all."

He tugged her close a second before crushing her lips beneath his. Strong, commanding, scorching, a sensual assault that left her reeling.

If their first kiss on the beach in Noumea had rocked her world, this kiss blew it into the stratosphere.

As she tilted along with the deck beneath her shaky feet, she realized she'd never been kissed like this, ever.

She clung to him as his tongue coaxed its way into her mouth, teasing her to match him. She moaned, a guttural sound deep in her throat, the noise inflaming him as he leaned into her, pressing her back against the rail as his arousal pressed against her, creating an answering response in her core, setting her wildest desires alight.

She should stop this madness, re-erect the barriers that had come crashing down the first instant his lips had touched hers.

But it felt so good to be desired, so good to have the attention of a man like him, so good to eradicate any lingering memories of what had happened on this night eighteen months ago.

His hands tangled in her hair, angling her head, as he slid his lips across hers as he tried to pull her closer.

Stunned by the ferocity of his need, she rotated her hips against his pelvis as his hand strayed to her breast, cupping and kneading, sending her resistance spiralling dangerously out of control. His thumb circled her nipple through the thick cotton of her dress, the torturous rubbing firing electric shocks through her body.

The sound of a slamming door broke the erotic spell and they tore apart, her breathing ragged as he ran a hand through his mussed curls, his expression dazed.

She'd lost control in his arms and she never, ever lost control.

At work, she was the epitome of control. Christmas parties, she'd be the sober one tidying up after everyone left. Farewelling staff, she'd collect money and choose the perfect gift. Organizing vacation rosters, she was a all over it.

All over Zac more like it, as her famed control washed away on the tide.

He laid a tentative hand on her shoulder. "Lana?"

"Hmm?"

She didn't know what to say, didn't know where to look, and focusing on Beth's indigo pumps with the gold wedged heel seemed a good start.

He tipped her chin up, leaving her no option but to meet his gaze. "I have absolutely no control around you."

She laughed, a brittle sound whipped away by the wind. "I was just thinking about control."

His hand hesitated, his thumb brushing her jaw before he dropped it. "My lack of?"

"Mine actually."

She hadn't wanted him to kiss her, hadn't wanted him to remind her of how good it had been the first time in Noumea, but since he had, she was glad. Glad he'd made her feel desirable and womanly and special for an all too brief moment.

"You don't have to say anything," she murmured, embarrassment flushing her cheeks. "You were trying to cheer me up, I get it."

He let another expletive rip. "If you think that was a pity kiss, you're out of your mind."

Out of her mind all right; out of her mind with wanting him to do it again and again and again.

"It wasn't?"

Shaking his head, he cradled her face, forcing her to look him in the eyes. "You have no idea what you do to me."

Flicking her tongue out to dampen her swollen lips, she said, "I think I have some."

Her wry response garnered a smile. "I thought you were immune to my charm?"

"There's no vaccination strong enough against you, Sailor Boy."

They grinned at each other like a couple of star-struck adolescents, the brisk ocean breeze buffeting them, pushing her toward him in an act from the heavens.

Over the past eighteen months, if a guy showed the slightest interest she'd usually flee, find a quiet place, and dwell on why he'd want to ask her out when she wasn't remotely date-worthy.

She hated that Jax had battered her self-esteem to the point she didn't trust her judgment anymore when it came to guys. Especially as she was the opposite at work. There, she'd never run from a challenge; she thrived on problem solving. She worked long hours by choice, tracking down the newest discovery, ensuring the latest display was eye-catching, cataloguing the backlog no-one else wanted to do.

She'd always been diligent: the model student who studied hard and didn't party, the devoted worker first in every morning, last to lock up at night. Good old dependable Lana. Reliable, steadfast, earnest Lana, which is exactly why she was here trying to build her confidence and convince herself a sexy sailor could just be a way to go about it.

Thinking of the museum brought her back to reality: she wasn't some femme fatale who went around inviting kisses from suave sailors on a moonlit night. She was career focused, her aim to reach the top of her field with a little more confidence, and should know better than to read anything more into a few casual kisses and Zac wanting to *date* her, whatever that meant.

She may be inexperienced with men but she was old enough to understand the purely chemical reaction when two people remotely attracted to each other flirted a little and that flirtation got out of hand.

"You're driving me to distraction." He ran a hand through his hair for the second time in as many minutes, more rattled than she'd ever seen him. "And considering the job I have to do this trip, I can't afford any."

"And you're telling me this because?"

He wound a strand of her hair around his forefinger and tugged gently. "Because despite every logical reason why I shouldn't do this, I'm struggling to keep my hands off you."

The wine she'd consumed at dinner sloshed around her stomach, rocking and rolling in time with her pounding heart as he tugged harder, bringing her lips an inch from his before brushing a soft, barely-there kiss across her mouth, a tender kiss at complete odds with the passionate kisses they'd previously shared, a heart-rending kiss that reached down to her soul.

When they eased apart, she couldn't fathom the expression on his face, the shifting shadows in his eyes.

"I have to go check on that fax."

"Right."

"Stay out of trouble."

With a brief touch on her cheek, he was gone, leaving her thoroughly confused.

Within the space of an hour he'd kissed her, comforted her, and bamboozled her. He'd been nothing but honest about wanting her, so why the sudden scram? One minute his kiss had been warm and gentle and caring, the next he'd made a run for it.

Ironic, considering she hadn't done the running for once. She'd embraced her newfound bravery and stayed, even after that scintillating kiss that normally would've sent her scurrying for cover.

But she was done with running.

If she couldn't handle a healthy dose of honesty—something he'd given her, even if the truth of how much he wanted her scared the hell out of her—how could she hope to become the poised, confident woman she needed to be at work?

She mightn't be able to give him what he wanted,

would probably disappoint him if she did, but that didn't mean she couldn't lighten up a little and actually enjoy his attention.

If she mustered all her meager bravado, she might even have some fun along the way?

## CHAPTER
# SEVEN

Lana spied Zac at the end of the gangway and sighed in relief. After he'd run out on her last night, she'd had her doubts about him showing up today. Crazy, considering she was the one usually contemplating a no-show.

Beyond impressive in uniform, she loved his casual vibe too: black board-shorts, white T-shirt, cap, and sunglasses shading his eyes. She wished she could see those eyes, read them, get a feel for his mood after last night. She hadn't seen him on the ship this morning, and while she was relieved, a small part of her couldn't help but wonder what he had planned for today.

Taking a deep breath, she headed down the gangway, half of her looking forward to the tour of Suva he'd promised her after she'd stepped in to save his butt at the aerobics class, the other half wondering how far her confidence extended when he started charming her again, as he inevitably would.

"I thought you'd stood me up," he said, his smile doing strange things to her insides.

Tipping her head forward, she looked at him over the tops of her sunglasses. "Why would I do that? I've been looking forward to the tour."

"I'm very good, you know."

"Ever heard the phrase 'self-recommendation is no praise'?"

He grinned and gestured to a small four-wheel drive parked nearby. "Come on, I have a car waiting for us." He bowed low. "Your chariot awaits," and pulled off his cap with a flourish.

"*You're* going to drive?"

She glanced at the chaotic scene on the dock: cars darting between pedestrians and street vendors, horns honking constantly as people jumped out of the way of moving vehicles in haphazard fashion.

He laughed at her horrified expression. "Don't worry, I've done this before. The car belongs to Raj, a friend of mine. He often lends it to me if I want to tour around. Once we leave the dock area and head out of town the roads quieten considerably."

Her doubt must've shown, for his grin widened. "Don't you trust me?"

"Your driving skills, maybe." She quirked an eyebrow. "The rest, not on your life."

He clutched his heart. "You're a hard woman. Now come on, get in the car before I change my mind."

She chuckled, surprisingly chill as they got in the car and headed out of town. She'd expected some awkwardness after last night but Zac kept up a steady flow of casual chatter as they wound around the island and he pointed out interesting landmarks. Content to sit back and watch the stunning scenery, she admired the sapphire ocean lapping at pearly sands, the beaches fringed by swaying palm trees, and wondered when she'd last felt this relaxed.

After half an hour, they stopped at a roadside café.

"Do you like Indian food?"

She nodded. "Love it. The hotter the better."

"Good. Raj put me onto this place years ago and I always drop in if I have time. They make the best chicken tikka this side of India."

"What are we waiting for? I'm ravenous."

As they entered the open-air café, the proprietor, a tall Sikh wearing a maroon turban, rushed over.

"Hello, Mr. Zac. Welcome back." He pumped Zac's hand vigorously. "And you have brought a beautiful friend. Welcome to Sujit's place, Miss."

Zac smiled. "Sujit, meet Lana."

He bowed over her hand. "Welcome. Now, what can I get you?"

She deferred to Zac. "You order. You'll know the specials."

"How about the usual, Sujit?"

"Most definitely, my friend. Coming right up."

Lana glanced around, surprised by the restaurant's cleanliness considering it was open to the elements. As for the sand floor, it would be a breeze to clean up.

"Adds to the island ambiance, huh?"

She nodded, surprised Zac could read her thoughts so easily, secretly pleased. "What's with the lack of table settings?"

"Wait and see."

"Very mysterious."

His mouth kicked up into a cheeky grin. "All will be revealed shortly."

"I bet."

He chuckled at her laconic response and gestured to a nearby table and she sat, savoring the spicy aromas coming from the nearby kitchen.

"Smells divine."

He slid his sunglasses off, the impact of all that dazzling blue rivalling the sky for vibrancy. "The last ship I was on used to dock here every week. I put on six pounds as a result. See?"

He lifted his shirt and patted his washboard stomach, and her mouth went dry. Those were some abs.

Before she had time to comment, Sujit arrived bearing platters of food. *Naans*, chicken tikka, *dahl,* and lamb korma were placed in a tantalising array in front of them and the delicious aromas made her salivate.

"Thanks, Sujit. This looks superb, as always." Zac smiled in appreciation.

Sujit nodded, his palms pressed together in a prayer-like pose. "Enjoy your meal."

After Sujit headed back to the kitchen, Zac glanced at her, a smile playing about his lips. "Well, what are you waiting for?"

Confused, she pointed at the table. "Plates and cutlery would be handy?"

"Those large, green leaves in front of us aren't placemats, that's your plate. Indian food here is served on a banana leaf. You just roll them up once you're finished and they're thrown out. As for cutlery, you're looking at it."

He wiggled his fingers and she couldn't help but notice how long and strong they were.

"Is that sink in the corner for washing up?"

He nodded. "Follow me."

As they soaped and scrubbed, his hand brushed hers

and she jumped, the innocuous touch raising an awareness she'd determinedly subdued since last night.

He stared at her, eyebrows raised, and she managed a weak smile. "I think our food's getting cold."

First to break the stare, she turned away, hot and clammy and out of her depth. Zac had shifted the boundaries between them with those kisses, had changed everything with his admission of how much he wanted her, and no matter how hard she pretended she could handle it, she couldn't cast off all her reservations.

With her head urging her to take a chance for once in her life and her heart terrified of the consequences if she did, she headed back to the table.

This was going to be a long day.

∼

Zac followed Lana back to the table, loving how she moved, all fluid lines and sinuous elegance.

Her long turquoise dress flowed from her shoulders to mid-calf, skimming curves along the way. He could see the straps of a bright pink bikini tied around her neck and he hardened immediately at the thought of seeing her in it. If the vision of her hot little bod in that one piece had been haunting his dreams, he could hardly wait to see her curves revealed in a bikini.

She'd pulled her curly, sun-streaked hair into a loose ponytail and he longed to reach out and wrap the tendrils that curled at the base of her neck around his fingers. He loved her hair, loved watching it bounce against her shoulders as she walked.

A vivid image of that hair draped over his torso and lower popped into his mind and he almost stumbled. This would be one hell of a tour if he walked around with a hard-on all day.

Determined to ignore his libido, he sat and pushed a platter of *naans* toward her. "Let's eat."

"Everything looks delicious."

"Wait until you try it."

He ladled a serve of *dahl* and korma onto her leaf, then reached for a *naan*. Her fingertips brushed his as he reached for the same piece and he clenched his jaw in frustration.

She hadn't done it deliberately—one look at her shy gaze firmly fixed on her food told him that—and he needed to get a grip before he made a mess of things like he had last night.

He broke off a piece of the soft, doughy bread, dipped it into the pungent curry sauce, and stuffed it onto his mouth before he said something he'd regret, like 'let's get out of here and let's get naked.'

"Mmm, divine." Her tongue flicked out to capture a drip of gravy and he stifled a groan, focusing on the unique blend of spices hitting his taste buds rather than how much he'd like to lick away that spillage.

He needed to say something to divert attention from how much he wanted her, to focus on anything other than the driving, obsessive need to get her naked and moaning his name while he plunged into her.

"Sujit whips up the best Indian food I've ever had. It rivals some of the feasts I've had in Singapore and India for authenticity."

"You've been around, haven't you?"

"Yeah, definitely a perk of the job. I've traveled almost everywhere."

"Any favorites?"

He'd steered the conversation onto safe ground, only to

be diverted by the small moans of pleasure she made between mouthfuls, and he gulped his entire glass of water before answering.

"Probably Alaska for its glaciers. I've cruised the Inside Passage from Vancouver and the ship usually spends a day in Glacier Bay. It's amazing that ships like ours that weigh around seventy-thousand tonnes can sail to within a mile of those monsters. I've been lucky enough to see huge chunks of ice calving off the ice face."

Maybe he should focus on that ice, focus on all that cold, anything to dampen the urge to leap across the table and drag her into his arms as she stared at him with wide-eyed awe.

"I also love the Mediterranean, especially Italy. Capri is great, with its ancient cobbled streets and home-made pastas."

He could've regaled her with tales of his travels all day, particularly as her wide, luminous eyes fixed on him with fascination, but the longer she stared at him the harder it was to forget every sane reason why he couldn't push their involvement no matter how much he wanted to.

He'd seen the devastation in her eyes last night, the lingering hurt from the jerk who had screwed her around, her desolation at having their relationship labeled a fling. He'd planned on backing away then but once he'd taken her on deck and couldn't resist kissing her, his plans to leave her alone had drifted away on the sea mist.

He wouldn't hurt her by having a fling, but couldn't offer her anything else considering where he'd be for the next year.

So where the hell did that leave them?

For now, he'd keep things light. He'd promised her a tour today, the least he could do after she'd come through for him with the exercise classes, and he'd make it a fun day for her if it killed him.

"You know, the South Pacific islands are growing in my popularity stakes all the time." He leaned forward and crooked a finger at her. "I think the present company has a lot to do with that."

She blinked as if startled by his compliment and he wished he could ring her ex's neck for battering her self-esteem to the point she couldn't accept a compliment without embarrassment.

"You mean Sujit? I totally agree, his food is to die for. I haven't been to those other places but I'd definitely put Fiji first on my list."

He grinned at her clever comeback but he wasn't done yet. "What about Noumea? How high should New Caledonia rate? I hear their moonlit beaches are magical."

The recollection of their first kiss stained her cheeks pink and her eyes dipped as he belatedly remembered he was trying to cool down, not get more wound up.

She pointed at the food. "You'll give me indigestion, flirting on an empty stomach. At least let me put a dent in this feast before you turn on the charm."

He laughed, more relaxed than he'd been in years despite his desperate yearning for her. It had been that long since he'd enjoyed a woman's company enough to spend more than a few hours with her, and while he dated infrequently, he'd never experienced such a connection on so many levels with any woman. Not even Magda, and he'd married her.

"Let's finish up and hit the road. I can't wait to show you the island's best beach. It's isolated, so tourists haven't wrecked it."

She mumbled an acknowledgement and focused on

her food as he wondered what he'd said to elicit that reaction. She'd been cool one moment, perspiration covering her skin in a delectable sheen the next, a sheen that had him envisaging all sorts of erotic ways he could clean it off.

If he were prone to flights of fantasy, he'd almost say she was hot and bothered about his mention of being on an isolated beach together. Yeah, and she wanted to rip his clothes off too. Definitely wishful thinking.

"Is the food too spicy for you?"

Her guarded gaze snapped to his, as if trying to read something into his innocuous question. "No, it's fine. It's just a little hot today."

Hot? It was positively burning, though the weather had little to do with it.

Sujit hovered near the kitchen and Zac made a sign indicating they'd like drinks—anything to cool down—and Sujit bustled out shortly after bearing two tall, icy glasses and a pitcher.

"Ever had *lassi* before?" He asked.

"No."

"It's made from yogurt. Very refreshing. It should cool you down."

While he'd need to dunk in a vat of the stuff to remotely cool down.

She took a tentative sip before gulping the cold, sweet liquid and running the frosted glass across her forehead, her eyelids fluttering shut as a relieved smile curved her lips. "That was good."

Maybe the *lassi* had done the trick for her, but he was about to explode, and as she opened her eyes he bit back a groan.

"You've got a milk moustache, right about there." He

reached out before thinking better of touching her and pointed to her top lip, his words strangled.

She laughed and wiped her lip. "Thanks. Not a good look."

He smiled and stuffed another piece of *naan* into his mouth, concentrating on his food as he mopped up the last of the curry with the bread, anything to take his mind off how much he wanted her.

As he topped up her glass and she drank again, he had the strongest urge to reach over, pull her head toward him, and lick the *lassi* from her top lip. Instead, he watched her do it, her tongue flicking out to caress her top lip in a slow sweep, and he almost bolted from the table.

"If you're finished, I'll take care of the bill and meet you at the car."

She nodded, the loose strands of hair around her face floating in the breeze, the urge to brush them away making his gut clench all over again.

"Thanks for lunch, it was delicious. Sujit's a great cook."

As he pulled out her chair, his hand brushed her bare arm and he gritted his teeth at the feel of her silky, soft skin. At this rate, he wouldn't be able to walk.

"See you at the car," he muttered, her open expression telling him she had no idea how much he was struggling with his libido as he turned away and called out to Sujit who appeared from the kitchen in an instant.

"Mr. Zac, your friend is special." Sujit's lilting accent held a wistful note. "You have known her long, yes?"

"Not long. Though I agree, she's special."

So special he'd given up a valuable day to be with her. After last night, he'd almost reneged on their tour; he could've spent his day off catching up on paperwork and following up that fax pointing to their suspected spy.

But wanting to cancel had been more than business; not only had that jerk of an ex done a number on her for sex, he'd lied to her, and the second Zac heard that he knew he shouldn't get involved.

Because he was lying to her too.

Every moment he let her believe he was a PR manager at sea he was being dishonest, and while saving the company demanded duplicity—and ultimately, making good on his promise to his uncle—it didn't stop him hating every second of his deceit.

So he'd told her a partial truth to compensate for his guilt, told her how badly he wanted her, expecting her to run at the mention of a date let alone anything else.

Instead, her response to his kiss had shaken him as much as the fact she'd stood her ground and hadn't run, and while he'd planned on begging off today, the memories of her fiery reaction had kept him up all night and drawn him here today.

"It must be serious. You have never brought a woman to Sujit's humble café before. Are you going to marry her?"

"No." A strange tingle ran up Zac's spine, causing the hairs on the back of his neck to stand on end. "I'm just showing her around your lovely island today. She'll be leaving the ship in a week."

"Ah, she lives in Australia. Why should that stop you from marrying? You also live there, yes?"

"Yeah, but she's a friend, and I'm not remotely interested in marrying her or anybody else for that matter."

Been there, done that, never forgotten the folly.

Sujit grinned. "Whatever you say, though trust old Sujit, he has a feeling in his bones about this one."

"You're an old degenerate." Zac settled the bill and shook his hand. "See you next time."

# THE CEO

"Maybe you'll both visit on your honeymoon?"

Zac chuckled, amused by his friend's one-track mind. Marriage again? Not for him.

As he caught sight of Lana casually leaning against the jeep, the wind whipping her hair away from her face while plastering the dress against her shapely body, all he could think was how much she intrigued him. He'd been attracted to her quick wit at the start, but now he wanted her so badly he ached.

But if they couldn't indulge in a fling, what the hell should he do? Back off?

"Mr. Zac, I've never seen you like this."

He tore his gaze away from Lana and refocused on Sujit. "Like what?"

"Distracted." Sujit pointed to his forehead, and imitated a frown. "Very serious."

That's because Zac's growing feelings for Lana were serious. Even the fact he was labelling what he felt for her as 'feelings' scared the hell out of him.

Sujit shook his head, his benevolent grin bordering on condescending. "I can see you're making this more complicated than it is. You like this woman, yes?"

Zac nodded, his gaze inadvertently drawn to her again, crushing need swamping him, blind-siding him faster than a swinging mast.

"Well then, do not overanalyse. Do not worry about the future and what it may hold. Live for the moment. See where the winds of change take you."

Zac stared at his friend as if seeing him for the first time, Sujit's words echoing through his head.

Could it really be that simple?

Was he overanalysing, thinking too far ahead,

projecting his fears from the past onto a possible future with a wonderful woman?

His conscience yelled a resounding 'hell yeah' and just like that, a mighty weight lifted from his shoulders and floated away into a cloudless Fijian sky.

"Thanks, my friend, you're a genius." He pumped Sujit's hand, his attention firmly focused on the woman who'd captured his heart without trying.

Sujit's grin widened as he placed his palms together and bowed. "I know. Now go."

Zac didn't need to be told twice, and as he headed for the car, refraining from breaking into a run, he knew the decision he'd just made had the potential to change his life. For the better.

∽

Lana squinted into the sunshine as she watched Zac stride toward the car. He'd been in a strange mood over lunch and the odd times she'd caught him staring at her it looked like he fancied her as dessert.

She'd had no idea how to handle the attention so she'd focused on her meal, steered the conversation onto factual topics, and muddled through the best she could. She hoped the vibe between them wasn't as tension-fraught at the beach.

"Ready to go?"

"Sure," she said, the false perkiness she injected into her voice garnering a curious glance from Zac.

As he drove along a winding coastal road and she took in the picturesque scenery, she replayed their lunch conversation in her head.

There was so much more to him than smooth words

and a charming smile. He was well-travelled, articulate, and self-assured, with a verve that captured her interest and engaged her mind. It only added to his appeal and she'd be better off remembering most of what he said was designed to tease her.

She'd fallen for slick words before. These days, a guy's actions would convince her to let him anywhere near her bruised heart.

"Wait until you check out this beach. I've seen a lot around the world, but I think this is better than some of the Caribbean beaches, not to mention Queensland's hot spots."

"I love any beach," she said. "My apartment's in Coogee so you can safely say I'm a bit of a beach babe."

"Well, you're right about one thing. You're definitely a babe."

Her measly ego inflated momentarily before she shot him a disapproving stare. "Oh yeah, I'm sure my designer wardrobe elevates me to babe status."

He paused, as if searching for the right words. "Don't take this the wrong way, but your wardrobe is a little—"

"Boring?"

Her deprecating answer had him darting a worried a glance in her direction before refocusing on the road.

"I was thinking more along the lines of sedate for someone your age."

"Which is?"

"Hell, I'm digging myself in deeper, aren't I?"

She chuckled. "Quit while you're behind."

She liked her clothes. They may be old but they were safe, familiar, like snuggling under a favorite quilt on a cold winter's day.

She'd tried a new wardrobe once before, a new look,

going the whole way with risqué lingerie. But none of it had made any difference with Jax. He'd hurt her just the same, designer dresses or not. Much safer to stay true to herself, to find a man who wanted her for the real her, not because of how she looked or what she could do for him.

"I like what you're wearing today. That blue brings out the green flecks in your eyes."

"My weird eyes change color according to what I wear."

"Not weird. I prefer alluring."

She snorted. "You could bottle that charm and sell it."

His bashful smile made her laugh.

"And I'm so *alluring* I have hundreds of men falling at my feet and it's all because of my eyes."

"You have one."

"Who?"

"I'm a male in case you hadn't noticed."

She'd noticed all right, was noticing more by the minute despite attempts to the contrary.

Fortunately, she was saved from replying when he slowed the car and turned onto a narrow dirt track. The jeep bumped and lurched over the rough terrain, as thick foliage slapped against the doors.

Thankfully, the vegetation thinned quickly and he pulled over in a clearing that overlooked an inviting stretch of white sand with an aquamarine ocean that stretched as far as she could see.

"Wow, amazing."

Zac's blue-eyed gaze fixed on her, bold and challenging. "Sure is."

He wasn't looking at the view and she squirmed under his searing stare, before he held out his hand. "Come with me."

She stared at his outstretched hand, wanting to take it, nervous he'd read too much into it.

He took the decision out of her hands by grabbing hers on the pretext of helping her from the car and she managed a tremulous smile, wondering if he had any idea what a big deal it was for her to hold hands with a gorgeous guy as they strolled toward a secluded beach.

Holding hands implied trust, implied dependence, implied she believed in him enough to lower her barriers; much more than responding to his impulsive kisses because of chemistry and the length of time since she'd last been kissed and the soul-deep yearning to be wanted by a guy.

As her feet sunk into the soft sand and he gripped her hand tighter, she knew her resistance to this charming man had slipped.

A loud caw captured her attention and she glanced to her right, at a huge bird perched on top of a towering cliff ending at the lagoon's edge.

That's exactly how she felt, standing on the edge of a very steep cliff, torn between wanting to jump into the warm, welcoming ocean below and experience the thrill of a lifetime, or let her feet fly for the predictable safety of the car.

With Zac tugging gently on her hand she had no option but to follow into the unknown with a man who had the power to unnerve her, while every self-preservation instinct insisted she should dig her heels in the sand.

## CHAPTER
# EIGHT

"Welcome to paradise," Zac said, as they stopped beneath a coconut tree, the air fragrant with frangipani, the view picture perfect.

"How did you find this place?" Lana murmured, reluctant to disturb the tranquillity.

"Raj brought me here with his family. We had a picnic, swam in the lagoon, lazed around. It's great being able to relax away from the tourists swarming the island." He breathed in deeply and exhaled, a small smile playing about his mouth. "I come back every chance I get, though I'm usually alone."

"So you haven't brought a horde of women here before me?"

Though she kept her tone light, she knew some of her enjoyment would dissipate if he confirmed he'd brought countless others here.

"You're the first." He squeezed her hand. "I wouldn't share this place with just anyone."

Uh-oh, more of that defence-shattering charm bombarding her.

With a nervous smile, she slipped her hand from his. "You can't resist the flattery. Aren't I the lucky one?"

He laughed. "Come on, let's go for a swim." He pointed to a row of palm trees. "Let's dump our stuff over there. I'll test the water while you get changed."

A great suggestion, as getting undressed in front of him would've made her beyond uncomfortable. Crazy, as he'd already seen her in bathers, but disrobing in front of someone implied intimacy. Besides, she'd taken another step down the confidence road today and worn the new bikini she'd bought in Noumea, and if the way he'd been staring at her over lunch was any indication, she'd be blushing from head to foot the first time he saw her in it.

She dropped her bag on the sand, whipped her dress over her head, kicked off her sandals, and rummaged in her bag for sunscreen. Just as she started to rub the lotion on her arm, he touched her hand.

"I can do that for you."

She squeezed the tube so tight lotion spurted out the end in a noisy raspberry. "I'm fine. You go ahead, I'll meet you out there shortly."

He didn't budge and held out his hand for the tube. "Unless you're a contortionist I doubt you'll be able to reach your back. This sun can burn you in less than ten minutes so let me help."

He was right but the thought of him rubbing any part of her body made the skin behind her ears prickle in that annoying way only he and strawberries could elicit.

"I'm fine, really—"

"Damn, you're a stubborn woman." He snatched the lotion out of her hand and squeezed a healthy blob into his palm, raising an eyebrow when she frowned. "Now why don't you play nice and lie face down on your towel?"

With an exaggerated huff she plopped on the towel, rested her forehead on her hands, and braced for the first cold dollop of lotion.

"I suppose you want me to thank you?"

He snickered. "You will."

He thoughtfully warmed the lotion between his hands, though his first touch was as shocking, as electrifying, as if he'd squeezed the entire tube onto her back.

She gritted her teeth and tried to relax under his hands while her skin tingled everywhere he touched. She'd never been touched by a man like this before. Jax hadn't been touchy-feely and his version of foreplay extended to a kiss and a fiddle down below.

She'd never experienced the luxury of a man's warm hands gliding over her skin in languorous firm strokes, and as platonic as this was, she couldn't help but enjoy it.

"You're very tense," he said, his voice gravelly.

"Must be the extra aerobic classes." As if.

He didn't ease the pressure, his hands stroking her back in long sweeps designed to be impersonal yet driving her mad with the sheer pleasure of it.

"Try to relax."

Easy for him to say. How could she relax when he was stroking her flesh, his strong hands splaying over her back, her defences unraveling as fast as her muscles unwound?

His fingers kept snagging the knot of her bikini bra, though she didn't dare suggest he undo it, for that would be *her* final undoing. She may be immune to his charms, but her long neglected body, was enjoying this way too much.

"Why don't you turn over and I'll do your front too?"

Just like that, her muscles twanged back to tense. The

thought of him rubbing her stomach sent heat surging to her cheeks.

"Not a good idea." She flipped onto her back and held out her hand for the tube.

"Why not?"

"Because I'm perfectly capable of rubbing lotion onto my tummy."

His eyes glittered and she shivered at their taunting glint. "But where's the fun in that?"

Her skin tingled some more and she itched behind her ear. "Give me the tube."

He held it overhead and waved it around. "Only if you ask nicely."

Clenching her jaw, she stuck her hand under his nose. "Please."

He chuckled and dropped the tube into her palm. "Actually, it'll probably be just as much fun watching you do it."

"Pervert."

"Just interested. But you already know that."

His low, suggestive tone had her squeezing too much lotion into her palm and, rather than taking her time to ensure she didn't miss any spots, she slapped the stuff onto her belly and did a few half-hearted circles before leaping from the sand.

"Right. Hope that water's warm."

"It's perfect." His heated gaze slid over her before meeting hers and she bit the inside of her lip to stop it quivering. He totally unnerved her, from his roguish smile to the devilish glint in his eyes.

He was toying with her, she knew it, but with every compliment she let her guard down a tad more. She wanted to believe him, wanted to believe he thought she was perfect. But she wasn't a fool, not any more. Objectively, how could he find less-than-a-handful breasts—another Jax-ism she hated—no waist to speak, of and thighs with the first hint of dimples, perfect?

"You're expression has turned, which means it's time to play, so let's swim. Race you there?" He flung the words over his shoulder and took off, tearing across the hot sand before she could move, and by the time she caught up he'd dived into the water.

"Not fair. You've got longer legs."

"Nothing wrong with your legs from what I can see."

Rolling her eyes, she waded into the cerulean lagoon, sighing at the blissful tepidity of the water. "If you stop laying on the charm so thick for a few minutes, I might actually enjoy this swim."

He pushed her head under water in response.

She sputtered and spit saltwater as she surfaced, clawing him, trying to return the favor, only to have him slip out of her grip. "You're in trouble, Sailor Boy."

They tumbled in the water for the next few minutes, arms and legs flailing wildly, laughing so hard she got a cramp.

She couldn't remember the last time she'd had this much fun. Her long work hours weren't conducive to play and when she went to the beach on the weekend she swam for exercise rather than leisure.

When they finally emerged from the water, she clutched her side. "You've given me a stitch."

"Good. I've never seen you laugh like that." He caressed her cheek, a brief, fleeting touch that had her fingers digging painfully into her side to stop from reaching up and pressing her palm to the skin he just had.

"That's because you're not that funny."

## THE CEO

"Ouch." He clutched his heart in mock outrage and she chuckled.

"The day I wound that enormous ego of yours is the day I'll go skinny dipping in the Pacific Ocean."

"I'm wounded, I'm wounded." He groaned and collapsed on the sand in a pathetic heap, writhing like he'd been stung by a lethal jellyfish, and she laughed.

"I'm going to dry off. When you've finished with the theatrics, I'll see you up there." She pointed to the palm trees and headed off, ignoring his call of "you're no fun."

She knew he'd meant it as a joke, a fly-away comment as part of their sparring, but the words echoed as she towelled off. She wasn't fun, didn't know how to have fun, not when she'd spent her whole life trying to do the right thing.

Beth had once called her a nerd and Land had shrugged, pushed her tortoiseshell glasses up her nose, and scuffed her flat heeled boots, agreeing with the assessment but hurt all the same.

Everyone saw her the same way, no fun: people at work, her cousin, even Zac, and while his opinion shouldn't matter considering she wouldn't see him after the end of next week, it did.

As he joined her and she watched water droplets run in rivulets down his muscular torso when he bent to pick up his towel, she wished her newfound confidence extended to having a little fun.

"I'm going to dry off in the sun for a while." And blink away the sudden sting of tears for feeling inadequate and inexperienced and inept, but she wisely kept that to herself.

"Don't be too long. These UVs can seriously burn."

She grabbed her towel and laid it on the sand a few feet away, an ill-chosen spot considering she had a clear view of him stretched flat on his back, and the perfection of his long, lean body, with abdominals composed of ridges of hard muscle.

Squeezing her eyes shut to blot out the tempting image, she must've dozed, for it seemed like an eternity later when his voice roused her.

"Excuse me, sun goddess, you should come into the shade now."

Her eyes fluttered open and she stretched, rested and composed. "Nice of you to be so concerned."

She picked up her towel and flung it next to his, ensuring enough space between them for no accidental contact.

"I'll admit my concern is altruistic. I don't want to rub lotion on you again."

"Why's that?"

"I enjoyed it way too much." His gaze trailed over her body, lingering on every inch he'd rubbed earlier and everywhere in between, and darn it if that prickly itch didn't start up again.

She quirked an eyebrow. "If you enjoyed something as mundane as rubbing suntan lotion on my back, you get out even less than I do."

He leaned forward, too close, too masculine, too everything. "Go on, admit it."

She bit her lip, inched back. "Admit what?"

"You enjoyed it too."

His grin was pure temptation and she waved her hand in front of her face as if swatting away a particularly bothersome fly.

"The only thing I'll admit to is finding your incessant flirting extremely tiresome."

His smile faded the same moment the sun ducked

behind a cloud, both leaving her slightly chilled. "Do you really feel that way?"

Her heart skipped a beat as she searched for a suitable answer. What could she say? That she didn't believe his compliments? That her self-confidence had been decimated by a guy who used slick words before that she couldn't trust easily? That she wished she could believe one-tenth of his attention was real and not some ingrained part of his charm? That she hid behind sharp retorts, using them as a barrier against her insecurities?

She couldn't say any of that so she settled for a semi-truth, feeling a tad guilty her barb had tarnished what had been an enjoyable day.

"Honestly? I'm not used to the attention."

He couldn't have looked more surprised if she'd stripped off in front of him. "You said things ended with your ex over eighteen months ago, but you date, right?"

Heck, look what she'd got herself into now. She could lie, but she'd always been lousy at it. Beth said her mouth pursed into a strange prune-shape the few times she'd tried it and she already had him staring at her like she was nuts.

"My last date was with a hero in a romcom on my streaming service."

He touched her hand and she flinched, silently cursing her reaction.

"I like you, Lana. And I want to get to know you better."

She shook her head, using her hair as a shield to hide her face. "What's the point? I'm off the ship next week so why get to know each other better?"

"Because it could be fun."

Her gaze snapped to his, surprised by the serious glint in those deep blue eyes. She'd seen him cheeky, teasing, even wicked, but nothing like the solemn expression fixing her with concern.

"Fun? The only fun a guy like you would be interested in over the next week is a fling. And I'm not."

His eyes darkened to midnight, disappointment flickering in their depths. "You don't have a very high opinion of me, do you?"

She shrugged, hating that they were having this conversation, hating she'd put a dampener on what had been a lovely day more.

"You're a guy. You're a sailor. You meet woman all the time. You're a master at flirting. The only reason you're paying me any attention is because of that stupid challenge I threw down that first night on the spur of the moment because I couldn't think of anything else quick enough to get rid of you."

She took a deep, steadying breath, clenching her hands to stop them from shaking. "It's nothing personal. I understand. You see me as some sort of challenge considering I'm not falling at your feet like the rest of the female population probably does. You—"

"You're wrong. Dead wrong." He leaped up from his towel and started pacing the sand, long, angry strides that showed he was wrestling with something.

"Am I?"

Her whisper stopped him dead as he swivelled to face her, before kneeling in front of her.

"Damn straight. Want to know why you're here with me today, on my one day off a week?"

"Go ahead, I'm sure you'll tell me anyway."

His hands cradled her face in their warm, firm grip before she could blink. "Because I like you. *You*. Not your clothes or your willingness to help me out or because I expect you to sleep with me. I like you because you're funny and smart and you make me laugh."

"So now I'm a clown—"

"Shut up." He kissed her, a soft, tender kiss that reached down to her soul, shattering defences along the way, scaring her beyond belief.

He eased away too soon, leaving her breathless and yearning. "Now, it's time to head back. And I don't want to hear another word."

She opened her mouth to respond that no man told her what to do, and he pressed his finger to it. "Not one word. Not another character assassination. Not another assumption. Not one word unless you agree to play nice. Got it?"

Her lips twitched and his answering smile made her heart sing. He wasn't asking for anything, didn't expect her to sleep with him, hadn't belittled her when he'd heard the sorry truth about her inexperience with men.

So what should she do? Spend some more time with him? Get to know him better? With the aim to...what? He had his life at sea, she had a great apartment in a hip city, a few colleagues she could call friends at a pinch, and a good job at the museum. They didn't have a future no matter how well they got to know each other.

"Stop overthinking." He held out his hand and for the second time in as many hours she silenced her voice of reason and took hold of it. "How about we go with the flow and see what happens over the next week. How much trouble can we get into in seven days?"

She raised an eyebrow and he grinned as a scary thought flitted through her mind.

Plenty.

CHAPTER
# NINE

Though Lana would've preferred silence, they made desultory small talk on the drive back to the ship. She could add excellent conversationalist to his growing list of attributes. She tried to concentrate on what he was saying, but she couldn't stop the thoughts swirling through her head, most of them focused on the man sitting next to her.

She'd never met anyone like Zac.

Confident and charismatic, yet astute enough to look beyond the surface and hone in on exactly what she wanted: a guy to recognize she had a brain, a sense of humor, and a yearning to not be taken for granted. She couldn't believe he'd been so insightful at the beach and cracked the protective shield around her heart with his sincerity.

So what now? She wouldn't have the guts for a fling no matter how far her confidence soared, couldn't do something like that unless she was emotionally involved. And while Zac said he liked her, like didn't equate to what she craved, a lifelong love from an incredible man who'd put her first.

Completely moronic, delusional, and crazy, but she'd been dreaming of her happily-ever-after for so long she'd somehow taken Zac's genuine niceness and tangled him up in her fantasy.

She cast a sideways glance at his profile and sighed, her heart hoping for a minor miracle while her head shouted wake up and smell the sea air.

"What are you thinking?"

"Not much."

"I can hear your mind ticking from here."

"If you're that perceptive you tell me."

"I think you're mulling over what I said back at the cove. Close?"

There he went again, being way too perceptive. "Don't give up your day job, you'd make a lousy fortune teller."

"Admit it. You're overthinking again."

"Nope. You told me not to say anything unless it was nice and I'm having a hard time coming up with something suitable."

His chuckles warmed her better than the sun's rays. "See, that's why I like you, every prickly, cynical, blunt inch of you."

"You like my bluntness, huh?" She sniggered. "I can't help it if you've been spending too long in this tropical heat."

He slowed the jeep and turned onto the dock. "You can hide behind that smart mouth of yours all you like but I'm going to get to know you better whether you like it or not."

"Yeah?"

He killed the engine and turned toward her, his slow,

sexy smile sending a shiver through her. "Yeah. Don't say I didn't warn you."

Charming sailor boy she could handle, single-minded sailor boy with a determined glint in his too-blue eyes had her plans to hold him at bay sinking faster than the Titanic.

Hoping her voice didn't quiver, she aimed for flippant. "I stand duly warned. Thanks for the tour."

"My pleasure. Hope it lived up to your expectations."

If she'd had any, he'd blown them clean out of the water with his shrewd observations back at the cove. She didn't want to get involved with a guy like him. But what if it was too late?

"The tour was amazing. Thank you."

"You're welcome. I better get this jeep back to Raj. See you at dinner?"

She nodded as she got out of the car, the thought of spending more time with him after the day they'd just had sending a tiny helix of joy interwoven with doubt spiralling through her.

He winked, and with a jaunty half salute drove away, leaving her head spinning and her stomach tossing with nerves at the many possible ways he could get to know her over the next few days.

∾

Zac pulled up out the front of Raj's and switched off the engine, wishing he could switch off his thoughts as easily.

Things were out of control. Or more to the point, things with Lana were out of control.

After lunch and his chat with Sujit, he'd been gung-ho, determined to explore the possibility of a relationship with her, despite the brevity of it. Then they'd talked at the cove and things had rushed downhill from there.

He'd known she was inexperienced but not dating? Hell, did that mean she was a virgin too? No way. She'd had that moronic ex—not that that meant much—and there was the way she'd responded to his kisses, the way she had a knowing gleam in her eyes at times. But what did that mean? That she had a bit of sass lurking beneath her prudent front?

He didn't dally with virgins. In fact, he didn't dally with women period considering it took all his concentration these days to perpetrate his plan.

But he wasn't fooling around with Lana, had known it the instant she'd made her true opinion of him clear.

He'd kissed her to shut her up, a kiss to demonstrate what she really meant to him, a gentle, soft kiss when he'd been hankering to devour her all day. He wasn't toying with her, so what could he do to prove it?

He got out of the car and headed for the house. Considering Raj's happy marriage and five kids, maybe his friend could give him a pointer or two.

As he reached the veranda of the whitewashed bungalow, Raj stepped out. "Hello, my friend. Had a good day?"

"Yeah. Thanks for the loan. I had a great time down at the cove."

"I'm sure you did. Sujit phoned me and said you had a beautiful lady companion with you today?"

He groaned. "I can't believe you two old gossips."

Raj's grin broadened. "He also said you were so besotted by this woman you could hardly finish your *dahl*. Must be serious. Care to tell me more?"

"Maybe. Though I'd kill for a cold beer first."

Raj shook his head. "Where are my manners? Come in."

Zac followed him in, waiting for Raj to grab two beers from a cooler before they sat in the comfortable cane chairs in the living room.

Raj held up his beer bottle in a silent cheers. "So, my friend. Time to tell all."

Zac had two choices: stay silent and listen to the hum of a ceiling fan or get an objective perspective on a situation that was complicated at best.

"Lana's different from anyone I've ever met. I want to get to know her better but I only have a week before I head to Europe. Not enough time to get involved."

Especially when the likelihood of her retreating back into her shell was high. He'd seen her growing confidence —the perfume, staying after the kiss last night, the hot new bikini today—but small changes didn't mean she wouldn't retreat at the first sign of an overeager sailor laying a possible future relationship on her after knowing him for a week.

He took a long slug of beer, savoring the icy brew sliding down his throat. "That's the short version."

"Do you have to return to Europe?"

He nodded. He'd let his uncle down once before, not this time. He'd make sure of it. "Jimmy's sick again. The cancer's back and it has spread."

Raj's bleak expression mirrored his. "I'm sorry. Is it—"

"Terminal, yeah." He downed most of his beer in one gulp, hating the injustice of a disease that had no cure and robbed a man of his health, his dignity, his life.

"How much time?"

Zac shrugged. "He's seen all the best docs in London and had varying opinions. Some say six months, some say a year max."

Raj grimaced. "Very sad."

## THE CEO

"He says he wants to be left alone, but I know the stubborn old coot better than I know myself. That's why I've signed on for the Mediterranean run for the next year. To check out a possible leak over there too, and to show him I'm taking an active role to set his mind at rest the company's in competent hands. And to visit him weekly whether he damn well likes it or not."

"Ah..." Raj nodded like a wise guru. "So this is the problem with your woman. She lives in Australia and you'll be based in London for the next twelve months?"

Zac braced his elbows on his knees and rested his head in his hands. "It's more complex than that."

"Matters of the heart often are."

Heart? Zac didn't want to open his heart to anyone, least of all a woman he probably wouldn't see again when she disembarked.

He leaped out of his chair and started pacing, wishing he hadn't mentioned Lana to his friend. "Why are we even having this conversation?"

"Because you, my bachelor friend, have fallen, and fallen hard."

Zac paused. "You know the biggest problem? I've lied to her and she's a straightforward, no nonsense person. She's been lied to before and it cut her up badly. How the hell am I going to tell her the truth now when she barely trusts me as it is?"

Raj's eyebrows shot heavenward. "She doesn't know your true profession?"

"No. You know secrecy's been paramount to give me access to the proof I'll need to convict our spy. And I only met her a week ago."

"For a woman you only met a week ago, you're sure doing a lot of soul searching."

Zac picked up his beer and slugged the rest, desperate to ease the dryness in his throat. "Crazy, isn't it? Happily single for years, then I take one look at this quirky, captivating woman and can't get her out of my mind."

"If she cares for you, she'll forgive you. Besides, it's only a little white lie. You do work on ships as a public relations manager. You also happen to manage the entire fleet." Raj chuckled, doing little to soothe Zac's nerves.

"I'm glad you find this situation amusing."

"You're really in a bind, aren't you?"

Zac rolled his eyes. "I feel so much better after talking with you."

"Sarcasm won't help, my friend. I suggest you go back to your beloved ship and think long and hard about your dilemma of the heart."

"Very poetic," Zac muttered, knowing all the soul-searching in the world wouldn't get him out of this quandary. The way he saw it, there was only one solution: tell Lana the truth and pray she'd be interested in continuing their fledgling relationship.

Though he'd never been a fan of long distance relationships, had seen them consistently fall apart over the many years he'd worked on ships, the thought of keeping in touch with her until he returned to Sydney, maybe seeing her on the odd flying visit, sent a thrill of hope through him.

"You know, between you and Sujit, you two old reprobates could start your own relationship counselling service."

Raj laughed, picked up the car keys, and slapped him on the back. "Come on, I'll drop you off. Everything will work out for the best."

Zac grunted in response and hoped his friend was right.

# THE CEO

～

LANA FINISHED her aerobics class under duress despite rave reviews from the participants. How could she keep her mind on the job when flashes of her afternoon with Zac kept popping into her mind at the most inopportune moments?

Take the rowing machine, for example: it reminded her of boats, which reminded her of water, which reminded her of beaches and ultimately Zac.

The treadmill wasn't much better: it reminded her of walking, hand in hand, to the pristine lagoon, with Zac.

As for her towel slung casually over a set of free weights, she wouldn't even go there, considering her skin tingled at the memory of his hands stroking her back while she'd been lying on her towel.

Thankfully, she made it back to her cabin without any more flashbacks, though once she set foot in the small space and closed the door, she slumped against it.

Of all the fish in the sea, she had to get hooked by a sailor.

She smiled at the pun, though there was nothing remotely funny about her situation.

She was falling for Zac.

There was only so much protesting a girl could do and with his non-stop charm chipping away at her defences almost twenty-four-seven, what hope did she have?

Considering he was a sailor and she was a landlubber, they had little hope of making a relationship work. Especially the type of relationship she wanted: husband, kids, noisy Sunday afternoons in the backyard rolling in autumn leaves with her brood, face-painting, playing tag, scoffing sticky toffee apples. The kind of childhood she never had. The kind of childhood she'd yearned for.

Beth understood. Her cousin wanted the same thing. They'd role-played happy families countless times as lonely six year olds when their moms had died in the same car crash.

Beth had found her happily ever-after and while Lana was pleased for her cousin, there wasn't a day that passed when she secretly craved the same for herself.

Winning this cruise and taking it had been a first. And it had been filled with firsts ever since: the first time she'd met a guy who saw beneath her prissy veneer, the first time she trusted a guy enough to get to know him better, the first time she'd felt real passion if his kisses were anything to go by, and she knew, without a doubt, that if the last of her defences totally crumbled, it would be the first time she fell in love.

A knock on the door made her jump and she opened it to find the man intruding her thoughts filling the doorway, looking incredible as usual in full uniform, the gold embroidery on his epaulettes catching the hall light.

"Hey, there," he said, his lopsided smile making her heart buck.

"Hi."

Why was it every time he caught her unawares her ability to respond coherently vanished as fast as her resistance?

She lowered her gaze, taking in his polished dress shoes, long legs in formal black trousers, and white jacket ending just below the waist. Handsome personified.

"How did the class go?"

"Great." If she discounted obsessing over inanimate fitness equipment and how they reminded her of him.

## THE CEO

"Just wanted to let you know I won't make dinner tonight. Business calls, but maybe we can catch up later?" He appeared oddly vulnerable and it made her like him more. "The ship sails at ten and it's a magical sight as we pull away from dock, so how about we meet under the Bridge then?"

She hesitated. Was spending more time with him wise when he'd said he wanted to get to know her better despite her resistance? Giving him the opportunity to chip away at her emotional barriers even more, to the point they could disintegrate once and for all?

Maybe it was the wariness he glimpsed in her eyes, maybe the hint of uncertainty tugging at her mouth, but he stepped forward and touched her hand.

"Admit it. You know you'll miss me at dinner. This way, I'm trying to make up for lost time."

She laughed as he'd intended, his charismatic smile disarming her quicker than she could say land ahoy. "Okay. I need to sharpen up a few barbs."

He squeezed her hand before releasing it. "Great. I'll see you there just before ten."

She watched him walk away, admiring his butt, her head filled with possibilities, her heart filled with foreboding.

How could their fleeting relationship end well?

∽

"Hello, sailor."

Zac straightened from where he'd been leaning on a railing, a poster boy for gorgeous nautical silhouetted against the Bridge, an appreciative gleam in his eyes. A misplaced gleam considering she'd worn a boring black calf-length skirt and an olive shell top which had seen better days.

"Glad you made it," he said.

"Didn't think I would, huh?"

"I had my doubts considering it's probably past your bed time."

She chuckled and waggled a finger at him. "Hey, I'm supposed to be the one practising barbs, not you."

"Maybe we can practice together?" His voice lowered as he wiggled his eyebrows suggestively, and she shook her head, unable to keep a smile off her face.

"You're hopeless."

"It's your fault." He sniffed the air like a hound, coming closer, too close, almost nuzzling her neck. "You're wearing that damn perfume again. Any wonder I'm bamboozled. Didn't I warn you that stuff was dangerous?"

"It's the only perfume I own."

Maybe she could blame the perfume for her gradual melting toward him? Ever since she'd worn it, her resistance had slowly but surely unravelled.

His low, sexy chuckle had her clutching the rail for support, all too aware her collapsing resolve had little to do with the fragrance and more to do with the charming man staring at her with desire in his eyes.

"Well, if you keep wearing it, you're definitely heading for a whole lot of trouble."

Heat flushed her cheeks and she gripped the rail so hard her knuckles stood out. "Oooh, I'm scared."

"You should be."

For one, crazy loaded second as he leaned toward her, she almost welcomed the danger of having a guy like him interested in her.

Clearing her throat, she deliberately relaxed her fingers

and straightened. "So where's this magical sight you promised me?"

"Be careful what you wish for."

His deep voice rippled over her like a silken caress and her knees almost buckled.

As if on cue, the ship's horn blasted as the massive vessel pulled away from the dock, Suva's lights twinkling like a fairyland as the ship sailed up the channel, a gentle breeze fanning her face, a welcome relief for her fiery cheeks.

She was no good at this. Even with Zac being so nice this afternoon, even with her defences lowered, she still couldn't throw herself into flirting unreservedly.

Introversion was a habit of a lifetime. She'd done it as a child, leaving her dad to work through his grief, then she'd done it as a teenager, flying under the radar of his countless girlfriends that waltzed in and out of a revolving door.

No prizes for guessing where her abhorrence of casual sex came from. Her folks had had the perfect relationship, their love for each other radiating out to include her, and they'd been the epitome of the happy family before that car accident had ripped their lives apart.

Her dad always assured her she'd come first in his life and she had. She'd never blamed him, because he'd mourned her mom for seven long years before dating again, but Lana never understood how those women could jump into bed so quickly when her dad made it perfectly clear he wasn't interested in a relationship, never understood what motivated them to be so free and easy with something she considered a gift.

"Well, what do you think?"

Her gaze swept the dock, the sea, before her eyes met

his, firmly fixed on her rather than the view. "You're right. It's magical."

His eyes glittered in the moonlight, and a sexy smile curved his lips.

"You're not looking at the view."

"I prefer this one a lot better."

She tensed as he lowered his head and his lips barely grazed hers, the feather-light kiss sabotaging her initial reaction to pull away, rendering her resolve to keep her distance useless.

He kissed her again and again and again, gently increasing the pressure with each kiss as a languorous heat stole from her lips to her fingertips, a heat she'd never experienced, a heat that stole through her body and into her heart.

He hadn't laid a hand on her, yet every inch of her skin tingled like he'd caressed it, their lack of contact only serving to increase the pleasure of their lips locked together, tasting, sampling, searching in an endless quest for satisfaction.

But she couldn't give him satisfaction; not the kind a virile man like him wanted, deserved, and she pulled away, wishing she had the courage to let go of her reservations all at once, throw caution to the wind, and see what happened.

"Definitely magical." He touched her lips—still quivering from the impact of his kisses—with a reverent fingertip, gently tracing the contours, undoing her one little stroke at a time.

She needed to reassemble her wits ad say something, but her mind wouldn't co-operate while her body reeled from the shock of his sensual onslaught.

"I take it that's part of your plan to get to know me better?"

She sounded too sarcastic and his smile faded as if she'd tripped a silent trigger. "Plan?"

She shrugged and wrapped her arms around her middle, chilled despite the balmy breeze. She had to be bluntly honest.

"You're trying to seduce me."

"Am I?"

His somber expression, the way his voice tightened, the distance he established between them by taking a step back, all indicated one thing: she'd insulted him.

Tugging on the end of her ponytail matted by the wind, she met his bitter gaze head on.

"Level with me, Zac. I may be some naïve recluse who hasn't been on a date in eighteen months but I'm not stupid. You said you like me. A guy like you has needs. So what I want to know is, why are you going through this game of charming me when there isn't a hope in hell I'll sleep with you?"

There, she'd said it, and while her gut churned with trepidation, her hands were surprisingly steady as she folded them in front of her before realizing she probably looked like a prim and proper nun and promptly released them.

A vein pulsed at Zac's temple as he raked a hand through his hair, dishevelled and spiked and thoroughly tempting, before he met her gaze, his clouded with disappointment, hers wary yet relieved she'd asked what had been bugging her since they'd met.

She'd had the guts to speak her mind and he had no idea what a big deal that was for her.

"This isn't just about sex."

Her eyebrow quirked. "Oh really?"

He jammed his hands in his pockets, shoulders squared, back rigid. "I meant what I said this afternoon. I want to spend time with you, get to know you, but I'll be damned if I stand here and lie about wanting to drag you back to my cabin right this very minute and have amazing sex with you all night long."

Her mouth dropped open, a squeaky 'oh' escaping before she shut it.

His eyes flashed blue fire as he fixed her with a steely gaze. "Do I want to have sex with you? Hell, yeah. But I'm not going to beg for it. If you want me half as much as I want you, you'll have to show me."

She bit her tongue, biding her time, trying to unscramble her brain long enough to answer, to give him a response half-way decipherable that didn't consist of another scintillating 'oh'.

Her hands trembled and her stomach rolled in time with the ship as it headed out to the open sea as she searched for the words to make him understand half of what she was feeling: confused, scared, excited, a mish-mash of emotions that terrified her as much as falling for this incredible man who pulled no punches and spoke the truth without flinching.

Honesty was all important to her, one of her top criteria in her perfect man, courtesy of the elaborate lies Jax had told to manipulate her. She'd never trust a liar again and here was a guy who was dead-set honest about what he wanted. She admired him for it even though the blunt truth of exactly what he wanted from her scared her beyond belief.

After a drawn-out silence, he reached out and she let him take her hand.

# THE CEO

"Look, I'm sorry for laying that all on you. But you have to know, you're driving me crazy."

"Totally unintentional, I can assure you."

His mouth kicked up at her wry answer and hers twitched in response. "Do you want me to back off? Slow down? Just say the word."

It was like being given a choice between a decadent double choc fudge sundae—something wickedly indulgent she knew she'd end up regretting later—and a single scoop of vanilla—plain, boring, knowing exactly what she'd get if she took the safe option.

Did she want him to back off? Her head insisted it was the logical thing to do considering she'd be off the ship shortly, but her heart was giving strange twangs it never had before, quietly urging her to take a risk for once in her sedate life.

Maybe it was her turn for a dose of healthy reality? If he ran, it wasn't meant to be. If he didn't...well, she'd face that frightening prospect if it arose.

Taking a deep breath, she went for broke. "I can't get physical with a guy unless I'm emotionally involved, that's just me. And I hate to break it to you, but I wouldn't have let you kiss me just now unless I'm starting to invest some emotion in us."

Understanding, stark and pure, splintered in his eyes before coalescing into a bright, hard blue. "I've kissed you before."

"Impulsive kisses. You turning on the charm."

"And tonight?"

After the time they'd spent together, after she'd grown to trust him through his actions—he hadn't pushed her for sex once despite his admission just now of how much he wanted it—emotion had more than clouded her judgment, it had taken over to the point she didn't know why she was holding him at bay any more.

She raised her eyes to his, silently imploring him to understand. "Tonight I've realized you've crept under my guard. And I'm starting to like it."

The first flicker of awareness in his steady gaze made her want to execute a perfect swan dive into the ocean. "You like it?"

Drawing on a meager reserve of resolve, she placed a tentative hand on his chest. "A lot."

He caressed her cheek softly, lingering for an exquisite moment. "Then where do we go from here?"

Damned if she knew.

∼

After Zac walked Lana back to her cabin, he headed for the one place he did his best thinking; the Bridge.

Ever since he'd joined the fleet as a young, eager sailor, he'd loved the control centre of a ship, the hub that drove these monstrous vessels. He loved the quiet efficiency of the staff going about their business, he loved the view, and he loved the gadgets. Hundreds of them that beeped and lit up and made his fingers itch to push them.

He usually popped up here on the pretext of consulting with the captain over something, when in reality he loved the buzz, the feeling of control he got because he owned this baby, and the decisions he made could drive her and the rest of the fleet further than the company had ever been before.

Ironic, considering he had no control over the situation with Lana. Or more precisely, control over his burgeoning feelings.

## THE CEO

He couldn't believe what she'd just told him. Sure, he'd caught the odd gleam in her eyes that indicated she was thawing toward him in the attraction stakes—not to mention her genuine responses to his kisses—but to say she was emotionally involved?

Hell. It blew him away.

It was exactly what he wanted, what he'd hoped for, to lead into a full blown long distance relationship, whatever that may entail.

The kicker was, she'd given him the perfect opportunity to say he was emotionally involved too, but he'd held back. For no matter how long he stewed over this, hashing out scenarios, it all came back to Uncle Jimmy and the fact he couldn't let him down, couldn't let the man who'd given him everything die alone.

Which meant he'd be on the other side of the world for a year, a whole three hundred and sixty five days, and he'd be damned if he expected Laa to wait for him for that length of time. She deserved more.

Besides, he'd traveled down this road before, with Magda waiting at home for him, and it had ended his marriage. She'd irrevocably changed while he'd been away, and there'd been no going back.

But Lana wasn't Magda and he owed it to her, and himself, to let her make the decision.

Rubbing a hand across the back of his neck, he sank into the nearest chair, leaned back, and focused on the control panel in front of him.

He had to give her the option, had to know he'd tried his damnedest to make it work with the quick-witted, infuriatingly shy, naturally beautiful woman. She was worth it, every unaffected inch of her.

He just hoped she cared enough to take a risk.

CHAPTER
# TEN

Feeling like a pawn in a romantic game of her own making, the last thing Lana wanted to do several mornings later was play chess, but she had a game scheduled with Mavis and she hated to let her down.

She sat on a comfy armchair and ordered a double espresso from a waiter, hoping the after-affects from yet another sleepless night didn't show. She'd had to use concealer to hide the dark rings under her eyes for the first time ever. Beth would be proud she even knew what the stuff was for.

Lana spotted Mavis enter the games room, the older woman wearing a cute nautical outfit—white pants, navy striped T-shirt with a neck tie, and jaunty red cap—and she waved.

When Mavis reached their table, she grinned. "Guess what arrived at my door this morning?"

"Let me guess." Lana screwed her eyes tight, pretending to think. "One of those dance hosts you're so fond of?"

Mavis roared with laughter. "Bad girl. Next best thing though; an invitation to the captain's cocktail party tonight. I'm sure there'll be a few eligible men there to bat my eyelashes at."

"You're supposed to be setting me a good example."

"Ha." Mavis snorted. "I think it's too late for you, my girl. You don't need any lessons if that happy glow is any indication. I take it your tour went well the other day?"

The tour seemed like a lifetime ago considering what had happened since. She'd mentally replayed the chat she'd had with Zac the night the ship left Suva over and over, driving her crazy. Luckily, Zac had been tied up with work since and she'd barely seen him. Maybe telling him she'd become emotionally involved was a good thing? Perhaps it had driven him away once and for all?

Indecision tore at her. She wanted to tell Mavis everything to get the older woman's perspective, but was still trying to understand the gist of it herself, so she gave her a brief version of events instead.

Mavis nodded in all the right spots, waiting until Lana finished. "Have you fallen in love?"

Lana sighed, resigned to the truth. "He's a sailor married to his job. What hope have I got?"

"Have you told him how you feel?"

"Sort of."

She'd told him she had feelings—of a kind. Invested emotion meant the same thing, right?

But they hadn't resolved anything that night. After she'd dropped her little 'emotion' bombshell, they'd talked around it, he'd made a charming comment, she'd fired back a quick retort, and he'd walked her back to her cabin. Besides, nothing would happen unless she had the guts to show him how she felt, he'd made that pretty darn clear.

"What does sort of mean?" Mavis touched a pawn and moved it forward by keeping her finger on it, frowning in concentration before moving it back. "Some newfangled term you young people have for chickening out?"

Lana chuckled. "Yeah, something like that."

Mavis glanced up from the chess board and fixed her with a stern glare. "So what are you going to do, Missy? You need to show him how you feel. Take a risk. See what happens."

Zac had said the same thing. She'd have to *show* him.

Would she have the courage to make a stand for the man she'd fallen for?

As she watched Mavis toy with the pawn again, a glimmer of an idea shimmered through Lana's consciousness, slowly coalescing into a plan that had her gut clenching with trepidation.

Did she have the gumption to pull it off?

Mavis cleared her throat. "Listen to your heart, dear. It's the only way."

Listening to her heart is what had got Lana to this point: confused, petrified, yet buzzing with anticipation. Ironic, as she'd always listened to her head until now. She'd been the perfect curator, the perfect cousin, the perfect girlfriend. She had a well-ordered, sensible life back in Sydney.

So why was she considering turning it topsy-turvy by getting involved with a guy like Zac?

Lana gestured at the chessboard. "Your move. Then I might tell you my plan."

"What plan?"

Mavis's eyes gleamed with delight at the hint of subterfuge and Lana chuckled.

"What time do you think you'll be ready tonight?"

"Well, there's a lot more of me to nip, tuck, polish, exfoliate, moisturise and pluck than you, so around six?"

Lana smiled and moved a bishop. "That's fine. If you

could meet me at my cabin shortly after, that would be great."

Mavis frowned. "But what's the plan?"

Lana leaned forward and crooked her finger, dropping her voice to a conspiratorial whisper. "I need your help."

∽

"How about this one?"

Lana glanced at the skimpy, thigh-skimming, crimson silk dress Mavis held up and shook her head. "I couldn't wear that."

Mavis shrugged and flung it on the ever-growing pile on Lana's bed, and picked another dress off a hanger from the quickly emptying wardrobe. "What about this?"

Lana took one look at the skin-tight tangerine tube dress and wrinkled her nose. "No way."

Mavis sighed and added it to the pile. "This cousin of yours sure has an interesting dress sense."

"Bold and brazen, more like it."

Beth had packed enough designer dresses to last Lana a month but every one she'd contemplated wearing tonight had ended up on the discard pile. And considering she'd have to make a decision shortly, her chances of finding anything suitable were rapidly dwindling.

"This one?" Mavis held a sequinned mulberry mini at arms length, screwing up her eyes with a thoughtful expression on her face. "The color is gorgeous."

As was the dress, the sequins shimmering like the finest claret as Mavis turned it this way and that. But the dress was super short, redefining the term mini, and Lana would never be able to pull off something like that without tugging self-consciously at the hem all night.

She wanted to make a statement, to show Zac what she wanted, not show him what he apparently wanted.

"Here, let me hold it up to you."

The second Mavis held it up in front of her and Lana glanced down and saw where the dress ended, she shook her head vigorously. "Next."

Mavis tut-tutted as she reached into the wardrobe again. "There are only a few left."

Lana's heart sank. She knew what was left. She'd examined every single dress at least ten times since she'd made the decision this morning to go all out tonight and prove to Zac she was ready to take the next step.

She always came back to the same dress, a stunning floor-length formal gown in the richest shot-silk jade, the strapless bodice embroidered with tiny emerald crystals designed to capture the light and draw attention to the bust.

The gown was a stand-out, the type of dress to make a statement, the type of dress fit for a princess, the type of dress to turn an ugly duckling like her into a rare swan.

But she'd baulked at trying it on, a small part of her terrified she wouldn't live up to a dress like that no matter how far she'd come in the confidence stakes.

She heard Mavis flicking hangers at a rapid pace, and knew the exact moment she caught sight of the dress.

"Oh my." Mavis clasped her heart, and drew out the jade sheath with reverence. "I swear if you say no to this one I'm marching out of this cabin right now."

Lana gnawed on her bottom lip, and twisted one of the few curls left hanging from an elaborate up-do Mavis had mastered with a few bobby pins and a squirt of hairspray.

"Well?"

"I like it, but—"

"No buts. This is the one." Mavis held it up to her and sighed. "Perfect. You should see what this color does to your eyes. That young man of yours won't know what hit him when he sees you in this."

That was all that mattered, really, what Zac thought, and the anticipation of seeing his expression when he first caught sight of her all dolled up and wearing this dress was incentive enough to make her reach for it with gentle hands and slide it off the hanger.

Mavis smiled her approval as she unzipped it with fumbling fingers, stepped into it and turned around. "Help me with this, please? I'm all thumbs and the last thing I need is to ruin the zip on the one dress I like."

As the metal teeth slid into place, Lana took a deep breath and glanced down, her eyes widening at her rather impressive newly created cleavage courtesy of the in-built bustier. If those didn't make a statement, nothing would.

"Right, my girl, turn around. Let's have a look at you."

When Lana turned, she caught sight of her reflection in the mirror behind Mavis, a second after her friend's mouth formed a perfect O.

"You're beautiful."

"Don't sound so surprised."

Mavis reddened. "I didn't mean it like that. It's just I've never seen you look—I mean, you don't usually wear—uh—"

"It's okay." Lana patted her arm. "I'm not a clothes horse, never have been, and I rarely wear makeup because I can't be bothered."

Mavis nodded emphatically. "Well, you're lovely without it."

Lana stepped closer to the mirror, and turned her head

side to side. "Though I have to admit, you've worked a minor miracle with this gunk."

The glittering moss-green eye-shadow and dark kohl elongated her eyes to catlike, the foundation created the illusion of perfect skin, and the whisk of bronzing powder gave her razor-sharp cheekbones and a healthy glow.

As for her lips, she'd gone for a neutral nude pink, nothing too over the top considering whatever colour she wore wouldn't last long if she had any say in it...

"All that goop has only enhanced what the good man in heaven gave you." Mavis held out a pair of shoes. "Now, put these on and let's get going before we turn into pumpkins before the night has begun."

Lana laughed and slipped on a pair of Beth's fabulous sky-high stilettos in a matching jade, took a final look in the mirror, and did a little twirl for good measure.

The emerald shot-silk sheath fit her like a second skin, the rich color bringing out the green flecks in her eyes, and for a girl who'd never felt beautiful in her life, it came close to describing how she felt at that moment.

"You're going to knock his socks off, my girl. Just you wait and see." Mavis patted her shoulder.

It wasn't just his socks Lana wanted to knock off but she wisely kept that gem to herself, though by Mavis's knowing look, she'd read her coy smile well.

This dress filled Lana with grit and determination, a woman ready to show her man how far she was willing to go, a woman with more than flirting on her mind, a woman willing to take a chance on an incredible man.

"Ready?"

Mavis held out her clutch and Lana smiled her thanks as she took it, before following Mavis out the door, knowing she was as ready as she'd ever be.

# THE CEO

Lana hovered near the entrance to the ballroom, watching the women in their designer dresses beguile their dates, sip champagne, and laugh without a care in the world.

She wanted to be like that—sophisticated, flirtatious, carefree—the type of woman a guy like Zac would want in his life, hopefully for more than just a few weeks.

But she wouldn't think about that now. Tonight was about showing him she wanted him as much as he wanted her. Tonight was a night for romance, for magic, for a shy girl to demonstrate there was more to her than shapeless dresses and baggy shorts.

With her heart beating in rhythm to the jazz ballad playing softly in the background, she took a deep breath, squared her shoulders, and entered the ballroom.

Her fingers convulsed around her clutch at the exact moment Zac caught sight of her.

Deep in conversation with another officer, he glanced up, shock etched across his handsome face before he mumbled something and strode toward her, his gob-smacked expression vindication her make-over had made a statement. Though by the reproach shadowing those cobalt blue depths, definitely not the kind of statement she'd expected.

When he reached her he stopped dead, his greedy gaze roaming over her before his steely eyes narrowed. "What's all this?"

At that precise second, Lana's world crumbled.

She'd imagined this magical moment all day, had built it up in her head to be picture-perfect, with Zac taking her hand, twirling her at arms length, before pulling her close and whispering how incredible she looked.

She'd imagined he'd take one look at her dress, her hair, her makeup, and know she'd done this all for him, to drive him mad with lust, proving she felt the same way.

She'd imagined him so crazy for her he wouldn't be able to keep his hands off her to the point he'd drag her out of this party and straight to his cabin where she'd finally shrug off the last of her insecurities and show what a little confidence did for a woman.

Never in her wildest dreams—or nightmares—had she imagined the cutting criticism underlying his question or the disapproval creasing his brow.

While her first instinct was to hitch up her skirt and flee, she wouldn't give him the satisfaction of knowing how deeply he'd hurt her, how she'd trusted him enough to do this and he'd rejected her regardless.

"By this, you mean the dress?"

His frown intensified as he glanced at her hair, her face. "And the rest."

She bit down on the inside of her lip so hard she drew blood, the pain of his disparagement slicing her heart in two.

Drawing on the last of her inner resolve, she concentrated on keeping her tone flat, unemotional. "The invitation said formal so I made an effort."

"I see."

Like hell he did.

For all his proclamations about getting to know her and admiring her intelligence and the real her, he didn't have a clue.

She had to get out of here, had to leave before her humiliation was complete and she broke down. "You know something? I don't think you see a thing."

His eyes widened, the electrifying blue brought into

sharp focus, and with his midnight curls slicked back and a tux accentuating his broad shoulders, he was breathtakingly handsome, a rakish pirate who'd stolen her heart and plundered her emotions without thought or feeling.

She didn't wait for a response as she rushed out of the room, making a dash for the heavy glass door leading to the Main Deck. She ran as fast as three inch stilettos would allow, ignoring the heavy footsteps racing after her, the wind whipping her dress against her legs as her feet flew across the deck.

She reached the Main Deck as Zac shouted, "Lana, wait."

As if. She hit a dead end, swivelled to the right, and her heel jammed as she pitched forward. Before she could hit the deck he caught her, his saving grip an instant reminder of how this had all started. Considering how it was about to end, she would've been better off sprawling on her butt that first day on the escalator.

"You're making a habit of this." His wry statement would've brought a smile to her face usually. Not tonight.

Silently cursing her clumsiness, she straightened, irrationally disappointed when he released her. "Was there something you wanted?"

*You*, she wanted the great seafaring charmer to say. Like that would happen after his reaction to her makeover.

"Why did you leave in such a hurry?"

Her disbelieving glare could've created an iceberg. "Why do you think?"

Her clipped response didn't alter his guarded expression. This was a waste of time and the sooner she made it to the sanctity of her cabin, ripped of this dress, and slipped into her comfy cotton PJs, the happier she'd be.

He dragged a hand through his hair, and muttered an expletive. "I've made a mess of this."

Also-freaking-lutely. And while every self-preservation mechanism insisted she make a run for it, she couldn't help but wonder why he'd reacted that way.

"What's going on? I knew there was something wrong the second you saw me."

His remorseful grimace didn't quell the rolling, rollicking waves swilling in her belly, making her nauseous while the three metre swells buffeting the ship didn't.

"I over-reacted. Your transformation took me by surprise."

Glancing down at her dress, remembering the shock of seeing her expertly made up face in the mirror after Mavis had worked her magic, she shook her head. "There has to be more to it."

"There isn't." He shrugged, his shoulders impossibly broad in the tux he wore as well as his uniform. "Don't you get it? I like the fact you don't go for all the artificial stuff most women do."

"You mean I'm plain?"

Ironic, she'd never felt so beautiful, so transformed, and he preferred simple old Lana.

Tipping up her chin, he searched her face for...what? Proof his opinion mattered to her? A telltale sign what he said had cut deep? Whatever he was looking for, he wouldn't find it. She'd become an expert at hiding her feelings from a young age, had fooled her dad into believing she didn't care about his string of women, had convinced Beth she was happy being a frumpy nerd when in fact she longed to be as gorgeous and confident and outgoing as her cousin.

"I mean I prefer the real you, the woman who captured my attention the first second she fell at my feet."

"You wish." Her mouth twitched at the memory of their first meeting. "Though I guess you're right, technically."

He trailed a finger down her cheek, soft, sensitive. "So what's with the war paint?"

"Don't you know?"

Surely her dramatic eyes, her contoured cheeks, and her pearly pink lips along with the sexy dress were enough of a sign?

Confusion creased his brow. "Know what?"

"I did all this for you." She gestured at her dress, her hair, her face. "To show you there's more to me than just a brain and a smart mouth."

His frown deepened. "But I already know there's more to you. You're a gym instructor for starters."

She had to tell him, all of it. Now that she'd fallen for him, hoped for a future with him, he had to know.

Besides, it wasn't like she'd deliberately lied to him, she'd just let him assume she was a trendy fitness freak rather than a boring, conservative curator.

"Actually, I'm not an aerobics instructor."

"What do you mean?"

"I don't work at a gym, I'm just a member."

His jaw clenched. "Then where do you work?"

"At a leading museum in Sydney. I'm head curator there."

His muttered expletive had her repressing a smile, considering she'd probably just landed herself in a big steaming pile of the stuff.

"Tell me you're a qualified aerobics instructor and I haven't hired someone liable to send my insurance premiums to the bottom of the ocean?"

"Don't worry, I'm qualified. It's a hobby."

He shook his head, as if trying to fathom what sort of crazy person would work in a museum all day then become an instructor for kicks.

Propping her elbows on the railing, she leaned back. This might take a while and when she'd bored him senseless, he'd probably jump overboard.

"I'll give you the abbreviated version. I was raised in Melbourne. You know about my botched relationship and when it soured, I moved to Sydney. Not just because of Jax but to get away from the mundane and start afresh. I wanted to try new things, do stuff outside my comfort zone so I joined a gym."

She'd never forget her first step class, when she'd slunk in wearing a faded blue T-shirt and a baggy leisure suit, and been confronted by twenty lycra-clad, designer fitness fanatics in fancy joggers.

"I made a sloth look good so joining a gym was huge for me. The bizarre thing was, I got hooked to the point I took an instructor's course. Not that I'll ever do anything with it —" he raised an eyebrow "—after this cruise, that is, but it was something I needed to do, something to build my confidence, something to chalk up on my quest to try new things."

Something shifted in his eyes—wariness? Hurt?—as she belatedly realized he'd probably add himself to that list.

"Curator, huh?"

"Yeah." She flicked her hair over her shoulder, not used to wearing it half down and softly curled with tendrils tickling her.

"I guess it fits."

He hadn't lost the brooding expression and her heart sank further. She'd hoped that by telling him the truth he might soften a little, understand where she was coming from. By the look of his compressed mouth and deep groove between his brows, he didn't.

"Fits?"

"Your image…before this." He waved toward her in a vague gesture, acute disillusionment making her want to rip the designer dress off and fling it overboard.

"Before looking like a woman who wants to impress her man?"

He shook his head, thrust his hands into his pockets. "You don't need to go in for all this fake stuff to impress me."

"But you said—" She bit her tongue, wishing she had more experience with men, wishing she had half a clue where to go from here. She'd tried to show him she wanted him by her appearance but he didn't get it. Worse, he didn't like it.

So what was her next move? Tell him outright? Yeah, like she'd have the guts to do that.

"What did I say?"

"Nothing." Yeah, she was a chicken.

He held her gaze, his eyes imploring her to tell him the truth, like he knew she was holding out on him.

But he hadn't reacted to her makeover as she'd expected. How could she stand it if she came clean about her feelings and he rejected her?

An awkward silence ensued before he shook his head and raked a hand through his hair. "I'm sorry, but I have to go. We've got a PR disaster in the making on our hands and I need to deal with it."

There was more: she could see it in the clenched jaw, the rigid shoulders.

"Worse, my work schedule triples in the final two days

of a cruise," he added, as realization dawned.

He was dumping her.

Before they'd properly started.

Stunned, she knew nothing could've prepared her for the sharp, stabbing pain cleaving her heart in two.

It shouldn't hurt this much, considering they'd done little but flirt and exchange a few steamy kisses. Some light-hearted fun. She'd made that perfectly clear right from the start. She'd got what she wanted, right?

Mustering the limited reserve of courage that had got her through the confrontation with her CEO when he'd told her she wasn't assertive enough to go on the Egypt jaunt, she effectively blanked her expression.

"I understand."

He reached out to her and her infinitesimal edging away had him dropping his hand uselessly to his side. "It's business."

"Business. Right."

The first prickle behind her eyes had her frantically searching for the nearest escape. She couldn't cry, wouldn't cry, and she'd be damned if she showed him he had the power to make her cry.

"You better go and take care of business." She turned on her heel and walked away, head held high, ignoring the impulse to hike her skirt and make a run for the welcome seclusion of her cabin.

This is what happened when she stepped out of her comfort zone, when she tried to be someone she wasn't; an awful, unmitigated disaster that would take her a lifetime to recover from.

She'd tried to make a big statement. Well, she'd done that all right. Pity Zac wasn't interested in reading the signs, hearing what she had to say, or anything else.

She bit her top lip to stop the sobs bubbling up from deep inside, hating the taste of the lipstick, wishing she could swipe a forearm across her mouth and wipe it off. But she was already drawing curious glances from passengers strolling the deck and she had a reputation to uphold even though her instructor contract would be fulfilled tomorrow.

Crazy, that even with how devastated she was feeling, she couldn't shrug her responsible work ethic, and the thought of returning to the museum next week, with sadness in her heart and no charming smiles from a suave sailor to brighten her days, a lone tear seeped out the corner of her eye and ran down her cheek.

Picking up the pace, she ran for her cabin, wishing she could run from the mess she'd made with Zac as easily.

~

Zac clenched his fists and shoved them deep into his pockets, torn between wanting to chase after Lana and jumping overboard.

Both options held the same danger: he'd be floundering way out of his depth.

He'd deliberately driven her away.

He'd seen the hurt in her eyes, in the tremble of her lip, and he'd felt lower than a sea anemone. But what choice did he have?

He'd planned on telling her the truth tonight, about exploring their relationship further after this cruise, but he couldn't do it now. Her little bombshell put paid to that.

As if the dramatic change in her appearance hadn't already set him on guard, the truth behind her move to Sydney sealed it.

She was a woman seeking change, a woman dissatisfied with her current life, a woman searching for something new.

A woman like Magda.

He'd survived losing Magda, had lived through the pain of seeing her change before his eyes, had hidden the devastation when she'd walked out on him in search of more than he could give.

It had taken him years to figure out they never would've worked even if he hadn't gone back to shipping. Magda had been needy, demanding all his attention, wanting to be the focus of his world. Their initial attraction had been powerful, all-consuming, and he'd mistaken it for love, had given up his career for her temporarily, would've done anything she asked in those heady honeymoon months.

But his folly cost him dearly, had nearly killed his uncle, exactly why he couldn't let Jimmy down now.

Though maybe he was being a tad harsh? Lana was nothing like Magda. She didn't demand to be noticed; in fact, the opposite. It had been her lack of artifice that had first drawn him to her, her natural vivacity a refreshing change.

Everything in his life was fake, all about 'show' for the passengers, yet Lana was real, so real he could hardly believe it. He felt good when he was with her, felt like his life wasn't a sham, especially with the current subterfuge driving him to distraction.

He wanted to feel that good all the time, wanted to cement their relationship and take it as far as it could possibly go. And after what he'd just learned, she had a fulfilling career of her own, a job needing her attention during those long months when he wasn't around if he took a chance on a relationship.

But should he? After tonight's metamorphosis, after what he'd learned, he'd be a fool ten times over to contemplate taking their relationship further. She was hellbent on trying new things, on boosting her confidence. What if he was just part of her quest?

She'd seemed so natural, so unaffected, so real, but did he really know her at all?

Unexpected pain, deep and raw, gnawed at his gut at the thought of not seeing her every day, not hearing her quick comebacks or her gentle teasing.

He'd grown to love the way her eyes lit up when she saw him, the way her lips curled at the corners when she was thinking, the way she blushed when his teasing hit too close to the mark.

*Grown to love?*

Hell no. He couldn't love her.

He wanted to test the waters with her, see if they could have a long-distance relationship without the complications of love and need and expectation.

Love complicated everything. Love tugged at his loyalties, making him choose between an uncle he couldn't abandon now and a woman who'd stolen his heart without trying.

But what if it was too late?

He loved her.

And he'd hurt the woman he loved, hated what he'd done to her tonight, all in the act of self-preservation.

She was special and didn't deserve to be treated that way. He needed to make amends.

Starting tomorrow, when he'd wrestled this irrepressible, overwhelming, surprising emotion into some semblance of control.

## CHAPTER
# ELEVEN

When the ship docked at Vila the next morning, Lana almost bolted down the gangway. Anything to escape a possible encounter with the man she could happily strangle with her bare hands.

She'd pegged Zac for a smart guy. But he couldn't be too smart if he hadn't read the signs last night, the biggest, glaring sign of all being her dressed to the hilt. Not that she'd be wearing that dress again. It now lay in a rumpled, crushed heap on the floor of her cabin where she'd ripped it off and flung it into the corner the minute she'd got back last night.

She felt like her old self today—almost, if she discounted a broken heart—in baggy Capri pants, loose tank top, and comfy leather sandals.

As for impressing enigmatic sailors into believing she was willing to put her heart on the line for them, never again.

She planned on having room service for dinner tonight to avoid Zac. Irrational, as he could find her any time he liked by waiting outside the gym at the end of her aerobic class, but she'd face that particular scenario if and when it happened.

Though after last night, she seriously doubted he'd be seeking a confrontation. He'd made that more than clear.

Touring Vila, the lovely capital of Vanuatu, proved to be a good distraction for a few hours but once she re-boarded, the jitters started again as she slunk from the staircase to her cabin, darting quick glances up the corridors in the hope to avoid him. She needed to get past this, get a grip.

With a muttered curse that rarely slipped past her lips, she fumbled her key before jamming it in the lock.

"I thought I'd find you here eventually."

She jumped, her heart sinking as Zac's deep voice rippled over her, still holding the power to set her pulse racing.

Determined to play it cool, she turned. "Was there something you wanted?"

"You know damn well what I want."

He had the audacity to try a roguish smile after what had happened last night?

Her eyes narrowed as she tried her best death glare, the one that got co-workers to do her bidding without a word. "Actually, I don't. I have no idea what's going on in that big head of yours."

"Big head? Now that's the woman I know and love."

Her heart skipped several beats before she realized it was a figure of speech. "I'm tired."

His smile faded as he reached for her hand and she snatched it away. "We need to talk."

"I don't think so. You made it pretty clear how you felt last night."

"That's what I want to talk about." He rubbed the back

of his neck as if he had a pain there; probably her. "All I'm asking for is a chance to explain."

She should send him on his way. She should ignore the tiny flicker of hope rekindling deep inside. Instead, her stance softened under the hint of vulnerability in his eyes, in his earnest, almost pleading, expression.

She held up a finger. "You get one chance."

His ecstatic grin had the corners of her mouth twitching in response. "I finally figured it out."

"What?"

"What you were trying to show me last night."

She bit back 'about bloody time', the confidence her makeover had inspired a crumpled heap along with the dress. She couldn't have this conversation now, not in the corridor outside her cabin. She could invite him in, a thought she contemplated for all of two seconds before discarding it as quickly as her makeup last night.

"When I told you how much I wanted you the other night, I said I'd back off. Until you showed me you wanted me as much."

Damn him for being so clever. She didn't want to talk about this now, but with his intense gaze fixed on her, she had nowhere to hide.

He touched her cheek, a brief, tender touch that conveyed more than words ever could. "I think you were trying to tell me something last night but I was too hung up on irrelevant things to notice."

His eyes searched hers for confirmation and all she could do was stand there like a dummy, wracking her brain for a quick comeback, a brush-off, anything coherent, and coming up empty.

Leaning forward, his lips brushed her ear. "I'm as

emotionally involved in all this as you are. Maybe more, and I want to show you how much."

His warm breath fanning her neck sent a shiver of yearning through her, his declaration leaving her in little doubt what he meant.

Heck, she'd always thought actions spoke louder than words and if they'd made a mess of things trying to articulate how they felt, maybe she should go for broke and let him show her?

Taking a deep breath and hoping her voice wouldn't quiver as much as her insides at that moment, she said, "Last night was a big deal for me. I was trying to make a statement, to show you I'm not just some mousy geek."

His hand rested on her hip, caressed her, then gently tugged her closer, his molten gaze an incandescent blue like the hottest flame in a fire, riveted to her lips.

"Mousy geek? More like sex goddess." He dipped his head, stole a kiss, tempting her, confusing her. "And you want to know what else I think?"

He cradled her chin, tipping it up so she had no option but to meet his blazing gaze head on. "I think you hide behind those old clothes of yours when inside is a passionate, exciting woman struggling to break free. A woman wanting to express herself. A woman who is driving me crazy with how much I want her."

With her heart thundering in her chest and filling her ears with its pounding, she could pretend it had drowned out his words. But it hadn't. She'd heard every single word, all of them true.

She did want to break free, to express the passion bubbling away beneath the surface, locked away where no man had untapped it.

Yet here was a guy who could do it, a guy who'd captured her imagination, closely followed by her heart, from the first moment she'd met him despite all protests to the contrary.

Here was a guy who could give her what she'd craved since his first scintillating kiss: fulfilment.

Mustering every ounce of courage she possessed, she stepped into his personal space. "My attempt at proving to you what I want last night didn't work as I intended, so how's this for a sign?"

She stood on tiptoes and brushed her lips against his, initiating a kiss for the first time in her life. And it felt great. Liberating. Incredible.

Zac moaned and grabbed her hand. "Come with me."

She clung to his hand, almost tripping in her haste to keep up with his long strides as they followed several staircases marked 'CREW ONLY'.

Wouldn't Beth have a field day with this, her conservative cousin being dragged off to a sailor's cabin?

She muffled a snort and he slowed. "Going too fast for you?"

"It's taken us this long to get to this point. What do you think?"

His answering grin held wicked promises she intended on holding him to as he picked up the pace, guiding her through a host of warren-like corridors before stopping in front of D21 and inserting a key.

"I know we could've used your cabin, but this way, you have the option of leaving any time you like," he said, stepping aside to let her in. "Because if it had been the other way around, I wouldn't have left your side until you booted me out the door."

Her heart soared and she wondered how she could've ever doubted him. To understand her enough to know this was a big deal, to know she might want to flee to the privacy of her cabin later if things got too much...he was incredible.

Reality hit as she entered the tiny cabin and her gaze riveted to the bed. She and Zac were about to make love; unreservedly, unashamedly, undeniably hot, sizzling, exhilarating, love.

He paced the confined space like a caged leopard, raking a hand through his hair and looking just as dangerous.

"Zac?"

He swivelled towards her, his expression torn while his hungry gaze roamed her body. "You sure about this?"

Heck no. What if she was lousy in bed, frigid, like Jax said? What if she disappointed him? Or worse, what if they were cataclysmically brilliant together and she fell further for him?

She fiddled with the neckline of her top, surprised by the flicker of irrepressible desire in the glittering blue depths of his eyes. If this daggy old top turned him on, he really must like her. "Nothing in life is a surety. We've got tonight, let's not waste it."

His lips curved into a deliciously dangerous smile as he held a hand out to her. "Didn't anyone ever warn you about sailors?"

Showing more bravado than she felt now the moment of truth had arrived, she placed her hand in his. "Yeah. Luckily, I gave up listening a long time ago."

He tugged on her hand until she stood less than a foot away. "You're one hell of a woman." He traced a line along her jaw, tilting her chin upward. "And I intend to make this a night we'll never forget."

Her heart slammed against her ribs and her pulse tripped in anticipation. "Show me."

Their gazes locked, the wild yearning in his sending a jolt of answering desire through her body. Her breasts tingled, her stomach went into free fall, and her knees quivered as he stepped away, his stare bold, assessing, as it raked her body, strongly seductive yet soft as a caress.

"Let me look at you."

Her breath hitched as he tugged her top overhead and dispensed with her bra with a deft flick, his sure hands making light work of the side zip on her pants too.

"I feel naked," she breathed on a sigh as his fingertips skated around her knickers—practical white cotton, unfortunately, considering being seduced by the man of her dreams was the last thing she'd expected today—toying with the elastic, excitement rippling through her.

"Almost naked." His sizzling glance from beneath lowered lids sent her self-consciousness about her plain panties evaporating along with the last of her nerves.

Zac wanted her. *Her.* Not because of her comfy clothes or boring knickers or quick brain and she'd never felt so special. If she'd needed a confidence boost, the adoration in his eyes as he scanned her body was it.

The air whooshed out of her lungs as he kissed his way down her body, slow, soft kisses trailing a path to her abdomen and lower, where she throbbed with uncharacteristic fervor.

She'd never felt remotely like this, had barely registered much pleasure at all during sex with Jax, yet Zac's lips, followed by his fingertips skating across her skin with finite precision, had her wanting to fist her hands in his hair and shove him where she burned the most.

"Yes…" Her pelvis bucked as he slipped one finger, another, under the elastic of her panties, caressing her folds, teasing her, pleasing her with a few simple strokes.

"May I?" He raised his head and she nodded, biting on her bottom lip to stop from crying out with the pleasure of it all.

With torturous patience he peeled her panties down, his hands stroking her legs all the way to her toes while easing her back onto the bed.

She squeezed her eyes shut at the sight of her lying open for him, naked, and tried to ignore the inevitable doubts that accompanied being this exposed.

She didn't have a supermodel body or big breasts or long legs. Instead, she had a hint of cellulite on the tops of her thighs and breasts that wouldn't win any wet T-shirt competitions. She'd always felt inadequate naked, had never felt sexy, and Jax had reinforced her insecurities.

"You're beautiful."

At that moment, with Zac's hungry gaze traveling over her, drinking in every flawed detail before his reverent gaze locked on hers, she almost believed him.

Her breath caught as he grazed her clitoris, once, twice, and she almost came before he lowered his head again.

She tensed as his hot breath fanned her, her hand stilling him. "I've never done this before."

His head snapped up, his shocked expression almost comical if she didn't feel such a novice.

"What I mean is, I've had sex but—not this."

She pointed at her nether regions, heat flushing her cheeks as a gratified glint turned his eyes electric blue.

"Then I'm proud to be your first."

With the first sweep of his tongue, any lingering resistance evaporated.

With the second, she clenched her hands to stop from surging up and digging them into his shoulders to hold him down.

With the third, her thighs fell open all the way and her eyes drifted shut as she savored the mind-blowing sensation sparking through her body.

This was all too much, too little, as he kissed her intimately, swirling his tongue, nibbling, varying the pressure and the rhythm until she exploded on a loud cry, sobbing with the sheer, mindless rush of it all.

"Are you okay?" He wiped her tears away with the pad of his thumb, so gently, so tenderly, she wept harder. "Lana, talk to me."

As he cradled her close she clung to him, burying her face in his chest where her tears quickly gave way to chuckles.

He stilled. "Are you laughing or crying?"

"Both," she mumbled, inhaling, savoring the addictive scent of sea air and Zac imprinted on his skin.

He pulled away and stared down at her in confusion. "You know, those are two reactions guaranteed to make a guy feel mighty insecure after what just happened."

She reached up and cradled his cheek. "Sorry, I'm overwhelmed."

How could she articulate what she felt, the gift he'd just given her?

He covered her hand with his and planted a soft kiss on her mouth. "You don't have to say anything."

Smiling, she turned her hand over and intertwined her fingers with his before lowering it, hoping he could read half of what she was feeling in her eyes.

"I want to say that what you just did for me—"

"My pleasure."

His wicked grin made her laugh, diffusing the tension and giving her the courage she needed to tell him the rest.

"I'm guessing by my reaction to you I'm not frigid?"

# THE CEO

He swore and squeezed her hand. "Who told you that?"

"My ex. The only guy I've ever had sex with."

Realization dawned, his expression thunderous. "So not only is the jerk lousy in bed, he blames his partner. Nice."

"I always thought the problem was me."

So the old adage of sailors swearing was true, considering the expletives tripping from his tongue at a rate of knots definitely made her blush.

He cupped her face and stared into her eyes, direct, compelling. "Listen to me. You're a vibrant, responsive woman and you drive me crazy. Promise me you'll forget everything that jerk said."

She wanted to believe him, she really did, but how did he know, considering they hadn't technically had sex?

"But we haven't—you know—done anything."

His lips curved into a delicious smile, a smile of promise. "The way you just responded to me, sweetheart, we've done enough."

No, they hadn't. If he made her feel this good with his mouth, imagine how exciting the rest would be.

With a coy smile, she met his darkened gaze. "I want you."

His eyes burned, hot and hungry, his answering smile pure devilry. "The feeling's mutual."

More emboldened than she'd ever thought possible, she slipped a hand between them, stroking his erection through his trousers, enjoying the shocked widening of his eyes.

Stilling her hand, he said, "We'll take things slow."

She didn't want slow. Slow would give her time to think and analyze and let old insecurities creep in. She didn't want to think, not now. She wanted to feel and savor and enjoy.

"Actually, I prefer fast." She blushed at her audacity, her

nipples hardening as she leaned forward and rubbed against the crisp cotton of his shirt, desperate to feel skin on skin, to feel all of him. "We'll go slow later."

"Whatever you want."

Her frantic fingers fumbled with his buttons, tripped over his ti,e and snagged on his zip, but the end result—a gloriously semi-naked Zac—was well worth it.

Her bravado halted at his tight, black boxers, her fingers trembling.

"Here. Let me." He shucked them and her eyes widened.

"Can I touch you?"

He nodded, his beautiful blue eyes heavy-lidded with passion, his gaze smoldering.

Her hand shook as she enclosed him, hard velvet pulsing in her palm, as she stroked him to the tip and back, easing down and up again, empowered, emboldened, decidedly wanton.

"You're driving me crazy." His voice cracked and high on her newfound sexual power, she knelt before him, eager to taste him, to give him half the pleasure he'd given her.

Before she could take him in her mouth, he knelt and reached for her.

"As much as I appreciate the sentiment, I want you so badly I'm not going to last five seconds if you do that."

She raised an eyebrow, delighted in his torturous expression as her tongue flicked out to moisten her bottom lip and his gaze riveted to it.

"Do what?"

With a growl, he swept her into his arms and tumbled her onto the bed, where her laughter quickly petered out as he lay beside her, the heat of his body igniting hers as he plundered her mouth.

Sensation rocketed through her as his tongue duelled

with hers, firing her blood, her imagination, and everywhere in between.

She whimpered as his hand slipped between her legs, her body throbbing and eager and yearning for another release as his fingers worked their magic.

"I want you inside me," she gritted out as she arched into him, clutching at his shoulders as the tension within grew and expanded and finally detonated on a shattering explosion into ecstasy.

He slanted a searing kiss across her quivering lips. "You can have me."

She should've been thinking about protection, thinking about the consequences of not using any, but with her body humming and floating on a plain it had never reached before let alone twice, logic had fled.

Thankfully, he rolled a condom on before rolling her on top of him, his gaze adoring as he gently pushed her up into a sitting position until she straddled him.

"You're incredible."

His hands skimmed her waist, drifting slowly upward to cup her breasts, teasing her nipples with the barest brush of his thumbs, sending aftershocks through her.

The faintest of spasms shuddered through her, the tension building again, coiling tighter and tighter, ready to send her into orbit this time.

She sucked in her breath as his hands spanned her hips and lifted her as he surged upward, thrusting into her until she cried out.

"You okay?"

"Never been better."

She clenched her internal muscles—scarcely used muscles—to show him exactly how much better she was with him inside her, thrilled by the flicker of shock in those endless blue eyes.

"You wanted fast, right?" He thrust into her again, harder, deeper and she gasped, her thighs quivering as he spread her a tad more.

"Fast is good," she managed to say as he drove in again and again, each thrust sending her closer to the brink, each thrust a lesson in exquisite pleasure, each thrust showing her exactly how great sex could be with the right person.

Though this was more than sex and she knew it.

But she wouldn't think about that now, wouldn't think beyond the earth-shattering spasms building, climbing, snaking their way through her pelvis and spreading outward until she could barely feel anything beyond the torturously exquisite tremors rendering her mindless.

Finding their natural rhythm, she picked up the tempo, glorying in his ragged breathing, his glazed gaze, his straining muscles as he pushed them both toward a climax big enough to cause a tidal wave to swamp the ship.

"Jeez..." She collapsed on top of him, stunned and sated and satisfied—very, very satisfied—savoring his strong arms as he cuddled her close.

"Lana?"

"Hmm?" She snuggled deeper into his chest, knowing she could happily stay here forever.

He ran a finger down her bare arm from shoulder to elbow, dipping briefly into the hollow before continuing to her wrist where her pulse beat frantically. "You're not frigid. And I intend to prove it. Over and over again. All night."

She whimpered, a low, desperate, needy sound as she clutched at his shoulders, hanging on as he flipped her onto her back and propped over her.

# THE CEO

"What do you think about that?"

She smiled, slid her hands down his chest, savoring the rasp of hair against her palms. "What are you waiting for?"

Zac didn't need to be asked twice.

He growled, nuzzled her neck, and smiled when Lana giggled, a pure uninhibited sound of joy.

She was incredible, the sex he'd been fantasizing about far surpassing his wildest dreams. To think, some stupid bastard had called her frigid, dented her self esteem, kicked her confidence. Little wonder she used to look at him like he was some kind of monster at times.

But not now.

Now, she gazed at him from beneath half-lowered heavy lids, her molten caramel eyes glowing with satisfaction, the green flecks glittering with excitement. She wanted him as much as he wanted her and he'd make damn sure he obliterated any last lingering doubts she was anything other than pure sex goddess.

"I'm going to do this all night."

Her breath caught as he licked a slow trail from the tip of her shoulder to her earlobe, where he lingered and nibbled.

She moaned and he tensed. He'd never heard anything so sexy and he could scarcely believe he'd just had mind-blowing sex considering his straining erection.

"Can I explore you?"

Her hesitant question had him wanting to sweep her into his arms and cradle her close, the hint of vulnerability in her soft tone enough to fell the strongest man. Considering he'd already fallen for her, all she had to do was glance in his direction and he was all hers.

"Go ahead."

Thrilled by her eagerness, he laid back, folded his hands behind his head, watching her.

Lust rocketed through him as she placed a soft, open-mouthed kiss on his neck, another one above his collarbone, before flicking her tongue out to lick him, a tentative flick that had him twitching.

He groaned as she nipped the sensitive areola, flicking a nipple with her tongue.

"Do you like that too?" Her tongue traced lazy circles around it, her voice holding more than a hint of wonder at his responses.

"Like it? You're driving me wild."

She stopped, raised her head, and sent him a smile that could've tempted Neptune. "Good."

"Is that right?"

He surged upward, his mouth seeking hers hungrily, needing her more than she'd ever know.

Her head fell back and her lips parted on a whimper as his tongue plunged inside, teasing and stroking, ravishing her in a deep, devouring kiss while his hands took on a life of their own, roaming and exploring her curves.

"You're so soft," he murmured against her lips, praying he'd have the control to make this last all night, as he'd promised.

For come morning, he had another promise to discuss with her, one he hoped she'd go for in a big way.

He slid his palms up her ribcage to her breasts, feeling the nipples pebble as her heart thudded beneath his touch. He knew his matched her beat, the rapid staccato rhythm sending blood pumping to every inch of his body.

She moaned as he skimmed his palms repeatedly over her nipples and she arched up to meet him. "Zac, you're killing me."

# THE CEO

He smiled, reached over to the bedside table, and grabbed a condom. "Not yet, but the night is young."

She smiled, gnawing on her bottom lip before holding out her hand. "Here, let me do that."

Surprised at her willingness to take care of the essentials, he handed it over, watched her rip the foil open, and finger the rubber like it was some priceless parchment. For her limited experience, she sure knew how to drive a man crazy.

Sweat broke out across his upper lip as desperate need tore through him at her first, tentative touch.

"How's that?" She unrolled the rubber slowly, every second a lesson in exquisite torture.

He groaned and stilled her hand, on the brink of losing control. Again. "Perfect."

"Good." She caressed his cheek, hooked a leg over his hip, and rose to meet him in an erotic invitation he was powerless to refuse.

He slid forward and entered her inch by inch until they were locked tight. He'd never known such a feeling of completeness, of being totally one with another person, and if he'd had any doubts that a long-distance relationship was the way to go, the fact she could be his soul mate dispelled them in an instant.

But for now, they had tonight, and he intended to show her exactly how much she meant to him, how much he hoped for the future, by making love to her with every inch of his body.

"That feels amazing." She arched into him, torching his body, rousing it to fever-pitch as he pumped into her, his thrusts setting her breasts jiggling, his excitement ratcheting up to unbearable.

She threw her head back, and listening to her soft,

urgent moans he knew she was close, as with each practiced stroke he took her to the brink.

He wanted to wait, to make it last, but with his own climax hovering, she screamed out his name and bucked into him, sending him over the edge as spasms ripped through him, a galaxy of shooting stars exploding in his head as he shot to the moon and back.

How had he ever fooled himself into believing this was just about intrigue at the beginning? The connection he shared with this funny, smart, quirky woman was real, unique, and so damn perfect he'd be a fool to let her do anything but agree to his plans tomorrow.

"You're incredible." He brushed a kiss across her lips as she snuggled closer, stunned by the ferocity of his love for her.

Damn, he needed space, a few minutes to reassemble his wits before he blurted his feelings in the heat of the moment and scared her. "Just going to the bathroom for a sec, okay? Don't move an inch."

Lana watched Zac, her gaze greedily roving his naked back, his butt, not in the least embarrassed.

After what had happened, what they'd shared, her insecurities had been well and truly blasted sky high. But it was more than physical, more than the cataclysmic sex, the exhilaration of being one.

Something had shifted between them.

She'd seen it in his eyes, a depth of caring that lifted her heart and transported her to a place of hope and dreams and beyond.

But she wouldn't dwell on emotions now. She had a whole night of snuggling in his arms to look forward to—and several repeat performances of the magic they conjured together.

Unable to wipe the self-satisfied grin from her face, she slipped out of bed to turn the lamp on the desk off, stubbing her toe on the way.

"Ouch." She grabbed her foot and hopped around, stumbling against the desk and knocking a stack of papers to the floor.

Managing a wry smile—looked like her clumsy gene kicked in even when he wasn't around—she scooped up the papers and several photos that had fallen out of an envelope.

Her heart stilled as she glanced at the photos, every one depicting Zac; in front of Sydney's newest high-rise business centre in a designer suit shaking hands with the Prime Minister, behind a huge conference table filled with international delegates, an old man standing behind Zac with a hand on his shoulder and a name plaque 'CEO, Madigan Shipping' in front of him.

Confused, she stared at the photos, a million questions buzzing through her brain.

Who was the guy she'd just made love to and given her heart to?

He stepped out of the bathroom at that moment, a lazy grin on his face as he glanced at the bed. However, his grin faltered as he looked toward the desk, what she held in her hands, and he blanched.

"I guess you have some questions—"

"Who are you?" She hated the uncertainty, the accusation in her voice. She shouldn't have pried, should've shoved the photos back where they belonged, but now she'd seen them she needed answers.

Running a hand through his mussed hair, he padded over to join her. "I own this shipping company."

"You *own* it?"

He nodded, managing to appear proud and bashful and ashamed all at the same time. "I'm the new CEO of Madigan Shipping. My uncle used to run the company, but he recently handed over the reins to me, though we haven't formally announced it yet."

She didn't get this. Why would a CEO be working on a ship he ran?

"So what's the PR stint all about? Trying to keep a tight leash on your employees?"

"Nothing like that."

He took a robe hanging off a wardrobe hook and offered it to her, and mustering as much dignity as an indignant naked woman could, she shrugged into it like a queen into royal robes, grateful when he slipped his shirt and trousers back on. She could do without the distraction while they had this cozy chat, though by the sense of foreboding clawing its way to consciousness, she knew they'd never be cozy again once they finished talking.

Indicating she take a seat, he perched on the edge of the bed. "The company's being fleeced, losing big bucks to someone in a high position feeding our trade secrets to the opposition. We're being undercut all over the place and I need to find the culprit and plug the leak."

He paused, suitably chastened. "To collect the evidence I need, I had to go undercover. This ship is new to the fleet, no one knows who I am other than as the PR manager. As far as they know, James Madigan is still the CEO, a distant figurehead they'd never connect with me."

She couldn't fault him for being dedicated to his job, to want to protect the company he owned. She of all people understood what it was like to be driven to be the best in their field.

But if he didn't work on ships any more, if he was now

stuck behind that great big desk she'd glimpsed in the photos...

"Where are you based?"

The instant he looked away, she knew.

He wasn't married to his precious job aboard ships.

He wasn't so enamored of the sea he'd never leave it for her.

He wasn't interested in her, period.

At least, not enough to have a real relationship beyond this fling or whatever it was they'd had.

"Where are you based, Zac?" Her voice had risen and his gaze locked on hers, regret mingling with an apology in those endless blue depths.

"Sydney."

"Right."

"Look, Lana, I was going to tell you—"

"Save it."

Turning her back on him, she slipped off his robe and yanked on her old clothes lying in a sad heap on the floor. A bit like her pathetic dreams of happily-ever-after.

She stalked to the door without a backward glance, had her hand on the handle before he crossed the small space and slammed his palm on the door.

"You need to hear me out."

Holding her breath, determined not to breathe in and let his heady scent, his proximity, undermine her resolve to walk out of here with what little dignity she had left, she turned to face him. "Actually, I don't."

He didn't budge. "I didn't tell you because I'm not based in Sydney over the next year."

She wouldn't ask him where he was going, wouldn't give him the satisfaction of showing a small part of her was curious, that a small part of her still cared.

"I'm onboard a ship in the Mediterranean, based out of London."

"How nice for you."

Her sarcasm fell on deaf ears as he fixed her with that steady, unwavering stare. So what if he appeared honest now? She couldn't trust one word falling from his mouth, not when he'd been lying to her the entire time.

She hated liars.

Jax had lied to her, had feigned interest in her to get the inside scoop on some precious artefacts he wanted to add to his private collection, had belittled her. He'd ruined what little self-confidence she'd ever had. But she hadn't really loved Jax like she loved Zac.

So what the heck would she do this time around to cope with the devastation of being lied to by another rich guy playing games to suit his own ends?

He dragged his free hand through his hair, his expression crushed. "My uncle's dying, he has a year to live max. He's my only family and he's in London. I owe him. I have to be there for him."

Her anger fissured, a tiny crack that allowed a modicum of sympathy to seep in. Why was he telling her this? It was irrelevant to the fact he'd still lied to her, had known there'd be nothing between them beyond this fortnight. In a way, heading to London made his treachery all the worse, for if he'd stayed in Sydney they might've had a chance.

"I was going to tell you, was hoping we could try a long distance relationship?"

She trembled as for one, infinitesimal moment she contemplated what it'd be like being involved with a guy like him for more than two weeks; to call him her boyfriend, to cross off days on a calendar, counting down the minutes until she saw the love of her life again.

But she couldn't do it.

If she couldn't trust him to tell her the truth when they were together, what hope would she have with him on the other side of the world for three hundred and sixty-five long, interminable days?

She needed honesty. She needed trust.

By his actions, Zac could give her neither.

With a shake of her head, she placed a hand on his arm barring her escape and pushed. "I'm not interested."

She didn't have to push hard as the second the words left her mouth, an icy, impassive mask slid into place, his eyes a cold, hard blue as his arm dropped and he stepped out of her way.

"Well, I guess I was just one of those new experiences you were so hell bent on trying this trip."

With soul-deep sadness clawing at her insides, robbing her of breath, she scrambled for the door handle.

"Hell. Lana, wait—"

She flung open the door so hard it almost fell off its hinges, slammed it behind her, and didn't look back.

## CHAPTER
# TWELVE

Zac sank onto the bed and dropped his head in his hands, the echo of the slamming door reverberating in his ears.

He'd screwed up, and made a major mess of things.

He should be hurt by Lana's refusal to contemplate a long distance relationship, should be smarting.

But he wasn't. He knew the score.

He'd seen the devastation in her eyes when she'd learned the truth, knew it wouldn't have hurt that much if she didn't love him as much as he loved her.

Every one of her responses, from the first moment he'd met her until now had been genuine, so there was no mistaking the depth of feeling simmering below the surface, the raw pain he'd seen in her eyes.

He'd hated hurting her, however inadvertently, had wished he'd told her everything from the start, but it was too late for wishful thinking.

A part of him wanted to give her space, a year's worth before coming back and trying again. He'd learned through his experience with Magda that if you love someone enough you needed to give them space to grow and change. She hadn't wanted that space but Lana would. She'd said as much with her quest for new things.

Maybe he should give her a year to do what she had to do, then re-enter her life and start afresh?

As pain rocketed through him, he knew he couldn't do it. He couldn't leave her that long, he loved her too much.

He was a man of action; prided himself on it. Business plans, mission statements, corporate policies, he could take a plan and turn it into reality. And that's exactly what he would do here.

He loved Lana, would prove it to her whatever it took.

And as much as he wanted to chase after her now, sweep her into his arms, cradle her close and tell her everything would be okay, he wasn't that stupid.

She needed time to calm down, time to evaluate what had happened here tonight. Before the photos, before the accusations, before the truth.

Simply, they were meant to be together, and he had every intention of making that happen.

∼

Lana had been summoned to the Bridge by the captain to thank her for taking the classes. Great, just what she needed. Instead of disembarking as fast as she could, she'd have to go through the final rigmarole of playing the dutiful employer.

What a crock. This whole trip had been a bust from start to finish and she wished she'd never won the darn thing.

Knocking at the door, she grimaced at her reflection in the glass. Lucky things had ended with Zac last night, because if she'd been plain before and he'd still been attracted to her, he'd swim a mile regardless if he saw the frightful mess she looked today.

Placing both hands against the glass, she peered into the massive room, and glimpsed a flash of uniform on the other side.

All those gadgets probably made a lot of noise and muffled her knock so she opened the door and stepped into the huge control centre.

"Captain?"

She heard a footfall, sensed a presence behind her ,and her skin prickled like she'd eaten a crate of strawberries.

A captain she'd never met wouldn't have that effect on her. Only one man did, the same man she never wanted to see again as long as she lived.

"I needed to see you, the captain was kind enough to do my dirty work."

"That'd be right." Her voice quivered as she turned and faced Zac, hating that after all the heartache, the sight of him could still reduce her to a nervous wreck.

"I need to know if I've missed the boat."

She stared at him as if he'd taken leave of his senses, glancing out the huge windows at Circular Quay on her left, the Opera House on her right, and the ship firmly berthed at its moorings.

He gazed directly into her eyes. "Have I?"

In an instant, she knew he wasn't referring to the ship. "What's this about?"

He tugged on his tie, totally skewed as she noticed he didn't appear the consummate professional for once, with dark stubble covering his chin and bleary eyes surrounded by dark rings. He looked as bad as she felt.

"I've been going out of my mind since last night."

She shrugged, unprepared for the swift stab of pain at the recollection of what they'd shared and lost last night. "You should've thought of that before you lied to me."

"Please, let me finish."

He sounded like a little boy asking for the last toy tug for his bathtub and though her head told her to run, her heart said stand and deliver.

"You shouldn't have discovered the truth by those photos. I—"

"It wasn't about the photos, damn it." She took a steadying breath, as surprised by her outburst as him. She never shouted or lost control. Not unless she counted the times he'd made sweet love to her last night.

He opened his mouth to respond and she held up a hand. "It's the fact you're based in Sydney, the fact you're mega rich, the fact we could've had more than two weeks if you hadn't let me believe—"

Let her believe he was a sailor, let her believe his precious job was all important, let her believe for one, tiny fragment in time she might actually mean more to him than a handy lay.

"Believe this." He swept her into his arms and kissed her, a divine, devastating kiss that demanded more than she was willing to give.

For all of two seconds.

Powerless to resist, she responded by softening her lips, allowing him access to her mouth, the logic of pushing him away shattered by the hunger of his kiss.

Her eager response shocked her more than the kiss itself and she broke away, dragging in breaths to clear her fuzzy head.

"Damn it, I didn't mean for that to happen." He raked a hand through his hair, adding to his rumpled state, and she clenched her hands, shaken by how much she wanted to reach out and smooth it for him.

Shrugging, she wrapped her arms around her middle to ward him off. "I guess it always came down to that for us, didn't it? A chemical reaction, nothing more."

"You're wrong."

Grabbing hold of her arms, he left her no option but to look up, and what she glimpsed in his eyes sent sadness through her.

Pain. A soul laid bare. A soul lost and confused and reaching out, just like hers.

"I didn't want to fall for you. I didn't want to get emotionally involved. But I did."

"Just not enough?"

His declaration should've had her running outside, vaulting the rail, and doing a perfect dive into the water, but it merely served to widen the gap. Too little too late, considering she could never trust him now.

"It happened to me once before. In my early days while I was still working the ships. I fell for a passenger." His mouth twisted into a grimace. "I fell so hard I ended up marrying her."

Shock speared Lana and she tightened her arms around her belly to ward off the pain.

"I gave up my job for her, left the ships for a year. I gave the marriage everything, paid her the attention she demanded but it wasn't enough. She couldn't handle my career when I went back to it, hated my absences. She changed. Her appearance, her outlook, her needs, her lover—"

Lana's gaze snapped to his, not surprised by the hard, unyielding blue or the sadness underlying his bitterness.

"That's why I over-reacted that night you had the

makeover. Another woman I loved changing before my eyes. Stupid, I know, but I'm a guy. We don't do emotions real well."

Her befuddled brain backed up a sentence or two, wondering if she'd heard him correctly.

He must've seen the confusion clouding her eyes, because he took advantage of her bewilderment by caressing her arms before his hands slid up to cradle her face.

"That's right. I love you. Whether you're a fitness fanatic or a curator or dressed to the nines or in nothing at all, I love you."

Her heart soared at the sincerity in his voice, the tenderness in his eyes. She wanted to fling her reservations to the wind and leap into his arms.

But she couldn't. It looked like her two weeks of being frivolous ended when the ship docked and now she was back in Sydney she couldn't shake her conservative ways.

"I appreciate you telling me. But what about the rest? Why didn't you come after me last night, explain all this then?"

Instead, she'd spent a sleepless night, alternating between cursing him, herself, and the great cosmos that had brought them together in the first place.

"Because I had to tie up loose ends."

"Loose ends?"

Her heart sank. She knew his declaration of love was too good to be true.

"As you know, I'm the new CEO of Madigan Shipping. When I ditched my job for a year to be with Magda, I didn't know my uncle was about to hand over the corporation to me. I let him down and because of ongoing job stress, he had a heart attack."

She touched his arm, sorry for his genuine regret.

"Uncle Jimmy raised me, funded my education, has been like a father to me and I owe him. And now he's dying..." he shrugged, pain pinching his mouth. "I've discovered our spy and set plans into action to rectify the situation, but I still need to prove to my uncle I can do this, prove I'm trustworthy, prove I can make his legacy the best in the business, and ultimately make this difficult time less stressful if possible."

"So you'll be based in London for a year?"

He nodded. "I'm afraid that's the non-negotiable part of the deal."

Perhaps her head still spun from his kiss and his declaration, because she didn't quite understand what he was saying.

"What deal?"

He caressed her cheek, his hand slipping to cradle her head, his fingers winding deliciously through her hair. "The deal where you and I give this relationship everything we've got, long distance or not. The deal where you use your annual leave to board the company jet and come visit your desperate boyfriend. The deal where I spend a fortune on teleconferencing and emails and every other newfangled way on the planet to keep in contact with the woman I'm crazy about. The deal where you can try as many new things as you want as long as you don't forget about your boyfriend pining for you on the other side of the world."

Gently angling her head, he slanted a slow, sensual kiss across her lips, a kiss that reached deep and soothed the parts of her soul that ached when she'd thought she'd lost him for good.

"That's the deal." He broke the kiss, and rested his forehead against hers. "Being the incredibly successful magnate I am, I won't take no for an answer."

She had to ask, logic demanded it, yet afraid of his answer as her heart dared to hope. If she took a chance on him, on them, and it didn't work, her confidence would take another dive and she'd hate that after how far she'd come. Not to mention how she'd handle a shattered heart.

"You have to know, this trip wasn't just about trying new things for me. I needed to build my confidence and thanks to you, I have. But what if we try the long distance thing and it doesn't work?"

"It'll work. I won't settle for anything less."

Her breath caught as he cradled her face, stared directly into her eyes. "I love you, I'll always love you. All the oceans in the world can't keep us apart."

Her heart expanded until she thought it would burst, her legs joining her hands in the shaking stakes.

"I don't know what to say..." She blinked back tears as his thumbs skated across her lips and grazed her cheeks.

"I think you do."

His lips brushed hers, slow, thoughtful, a soul-reaching kiss that coaxed her into believing this was happening and this was real.

"I love you too," she breathed on a sigh, clinging to him, powerless to do anything other than love this incredibly impressive man.

As he let out a jubilant whoop louder than the ship's horn she kissed him with all the passion, love, and adoration she'd been storing away for a few days now, ever since she'd realized the terrifying truth: that she would never love another man as much as she loved him.

"I love you so much, sweetheart. Don't you ever run out

on me again. Last night was the longest, loneliest night of my life."

"Same here." Snuggling into him, she breathed in his sinfully addictive scent, stunned she'd get to savor it for the rest of her life.

He nuzzled her neck and she squealed as he nipped her, his lips searing a trail toward her mouth as heat flooded her body, a predictable response as she swayed toward him.

It had been like this right from the start, her body knowing on some instinctual level he was the man for her, while her head took a while to process the idea.

Zac loved her, this powerful, commanding, sexy guy loved her.

Life couldn't get any better.

"You know, I could always see if one of the London museums could do with a top notch curator."

He eased away, shock widening his eyes to endless blue proportions. "You'd do that for me?"

"Only if you're good."

With the same wicked smile he'd used to charm her from day one, he wrapped his arms around her, stroked her back, set her body ablaze.

"Oh, I'm better than good. I'm brilliant."

"That's a pretty high recommendation to live up to, Sailor Boy."

"Care to help me try?"

"Aye, aye," she murmured, as his lips lowered to hers.

# FREE BOOK AND MORE

SIGN UP TO NICOLA'S NEWSLETTER for a free book!

Read Nicola's newest feel-good romance **DID NOT FINISH**

Or her new gothic **THE RETREAT**

Try the **BASHFUL BRIDES** series

NOT THE MARRYING KIND

NOT THE ROMANTIC KIND

NOT THE DARING KIND

NOT THE DATING KIND

The **WORKPLACE LIAISONS** series

THE BOSS

THE CEO

The **CREATIVE IN LOVE** series

THE GRUMPY GUY

THE SHY GUY

THE GOOD GUY

Try the **BOMBSHELLS** series

BEFORE (FREE!)

BRASH

BLUSH

BOLD

BAD

BOMBSHELLS BOXED SET

The **WORLD APART** series

WALKING THE LINE (FREE!)

CROSSING THE LINE

TOWING THE LINE

BLURRING THE LINE

WORLD APART BOXED SET

The **HOT ISLAND NIGHTS** duo

WICKED NIGHTS

WANTON NIGHTS

The **BOLLYWOOD BILLIONAIRES** series

FAKING IT

MAKING IT

The **LOOKING FOR LOVE** series

LUCKY LOVE

CRAZY LOVE

SAPPHIRES ARE A GUY'S BEST FRIEND

THE SECOND CHANCE GUY

Check out Nicola's website for a full list of her books.

**And read her other romances as Nikki North.**

**'MILLIONAIRE IN THE CITY'** series.

LUCKY

COCKY

CRAZY

FANCY

FLIRTY

FOLLY

MADLY

Check out the **ESCAPE WITH ME** series.

DATE ME

LOVE ME

DARE ME

TRUST ME

FORGIVE ME

Try the **LAW BREAKER** series

THE DEAL MAKER

THE CONTRACT BREAKER

# About the Author

USA TODAY bestselling and multi-award winning author Nicola Marsh writes page-turning fiction to keep you up all night.
She's published 80 books and sold 8 million copies worldwide.
She currently writes contemporary romance and domestic suspense.
She's also a Waldenbooks, Bookscan, Amazon, iBooks and Barnes & Noble bestseller, a RBY (Romantic Book of the Year) and National Readers' Choice Award winner, and a multi-finalist for a number of awards including the Romantic Times Reviewers' Choice Award, HOLT Medallion, Booksellers' Best, Golden Quill, Laurel Wreath, and More than Magic.
A physiotherapist for thirteen years, she now adores writing full time, raising her two dashing young heroes, sharing fine food with family and friends, and her favorite, curling up with a good book!